AYE, AYE, SIR!

AYE, AYE, SIR!

By La Rocque Du Bose

ILLUSTRATED BY MILLARD MC GEE

Lothrop, Lee & Shepard Co., Inc.

NEW YORK

FOR
MY TWO
E. G. D.'s

FOREWORD

In the early spring of the year 1783, Captain Henry Wilson and his young son, Henry, Jr., set sail from Plymouth, England, in the *Antelope*, bound for Macao on the China coast.

The *Antelope* was a sturdy, three-hundred-ton packet ship belonging to the East India Company, and everyone aboard was confident that this would be just another routine voyage.

This book is the story of that exciting adventure, and except for a few minor details which have been changed, it is all true.

AYE, AYE, SIR!

1

Henry Wilson stood on the bridge of the ship until the dock and the people on it were lost to view. Then he made his way slowly to his father's cabin. Captain Wilson was looking over some charts when his son entered.

"Henry," he said, motioning to the chair beside his desk, "sit down."

The captain rolled up the charts and put them on the shelf behind him. Then he turned back to face his son.

"Henry, you know you are going with me only because the midshipman who was to have made this voyage died yesterday of smallpox. You must do the job as well as he would have done it—and that is what I wanted to talk to you about."

The captain leaned forward. "You are my son," he said, "but you are now a midshipman in my crew. If you shirk your duty or do your work carelessly, you will receive what punishment you deserve, and I shan't raise a finger to stop it.

"As a midshipman, you may give orders to no one. You will receive orders from *any* officer, and those orders must be carried out to the letter. If the ship gets into any trouble, you will be called upon to do things which you may not think yourself capable of doing, but you will do them. Do I make myself clear, *Mister* Wilson?"

"Yes, Father," said Henry.

"Yes, *what?*" said the captain, sternly.

"I mean, yes, *Captain*," said Henry quickly.

"That's better. You will eat in the officer's mess, and you will sleep in the midshipmen's quarters, and I think you had better put your things away now so that you can eat soon. You will stand your first watch on deck from twelve until four o'clock."

"Yes, sir." Henry started toward the cabin door.

"Mister Wilson," called the captain.

"Yes, sir?" said Henry, turning.

Captain Wilson walked around his desk. He reached out and took his son's hand in his own and shook it with a firm, man-to-man grip. "Glad to have you aboard, sir," said the captain, smiling.

8

"Thank you, Captain," said Henry, seriously. "Glad to be aboard."

When he was about halfway from his father's cabin to the midshipmen's quarters, Henry stopped in the passageway and leaned against the wall, or bulkhead, as it is called on a ship. For a few moments he thought about what his father had said to him in the cabin. He knew that the captain was right, of course. If his father showed him any favoritism, the rest of the crew would be quick to spot it, and would just as quickly lose their respect for Captain Wilson. And, as Henry well knew from stories which his father had told him, the captain whose crew does not respect him is bound for serious trouble.

With these thoughts going through his mind, Henry entered the midshipmen's quarters, a small cubbyhole just large enough for three bunks. Robert White, one of the midshipmen, was lying on his bunk, but he got up as Henry came into the room.

"Hello," said Henry, extending his hand. "I'm Henry Wilson."

White shook Henry's hand vigorously. "Very happy to meet you, Captain," he said. "I am Lord Nelson."

"No, you don't understand," said Henry. "I'm Henry Wilson, *Junior*."

"Oh, the captain's *son*," said Robert, smiling. "Well, in that case, I am Robert White—and I'm still very happy to meet you. Is this your first voyage?"

"Yes," said Henry. "Oh, I went to Portugal with my father once, but this is my first trip as a midshipman. Is it your first?"

"No, it's the fourth," said Robert. "I went to Portugal,

too, on my first one, two years ago, and since then I've been to America and Cape Town."

"Well, it looks as if I'm the only one aboard who has no experience," said Henry.

"Oh? Has Sharp been out before?" asked Robert, referring to the other midshipman in the crew.

"Yes, this is his third," said Henry.

"Really?" said White, surprised. "He doesn't look old enough to have been out twice before."

"Well," said Henry, "he says he has, but he wouldn't tell me where he'd been. Where is he now?"

"He's on deck," said White. "He had the first watch." He paused for a moment, and then said, "I take it you don't care much for Mr. Sharp."

This was true. Richard Sharp had begun by asking with a sneer, "Have you ever been to sea?" And when Henry said yes, he said, "How many times?"

"Only once. But . . ."

"There! You see!" interrupted Richard. "You haven't been as many places as I have. And where did you go on your one voyage, *lad*?"

Henry had gritted his teeth, determined not to lose his temper. "To Portugal," he said. "Where did you go on yours?"

"None of your business," said Richard.

At that moment, Henry had heard his father calling. He looked at Richard and said furiously, "I'll find out where you went. You've probably done no more than make two trips across the Channel to Dunkirk!"

But now Henry smiled and merely said to Robert, "I'm afraid we didn't get along too well when we met."

10

"I can understand that," said White. "I've only known him a day or two, and I've taken a disliking to him, too. When did you meet him?"

"I was at the dock when we loaded," Henry explained. "Then I went with my father and the cook to buy the rest of our supplies."

He went on to say he could never get used to the idea of buying food in such large amounts—a hundred dozen eggs, a ton of flour. Then there were sheep and goats and even cows to be bought. Their milk would be used at first, and then their meat, so that they served a double purpose.

Making certain that there would be sufficient food and other necessities on hand to keep thirty-three men fed and reasonably comfortable for three or four months was no small job.

Food had to be purchased very carefully, so that neither the money spent to buy it nor the space used to store it would be wasted. If lettuce could be kept fresh for only nine days, and if each of the thirty-three men could be expected to eat an average of one head of lettuce every three days, then ninety-nine heads of lettuce were all that they would buy—for every inch of space aboard a ship was precious.

"And now," said Henry, "I'd like to ask you some questions. I don't know what I'm supposed to do as a midshipman."

They sat on their bunks. "There's not much to it at first," said Robert. "You simply stand watch on the quarterdeck and observe everything that goes on. If an extra man is needed on a job, you're expected to help.

11

They will probably send you up to the crow's nest pretty soon, and later they'll let you take the wheel to see if you can steer straight. That's about all there is to it."

"I see," said Henry, doubtfully. "It doesn't sound too difficult."

"It isn't," said Robert reassuringly. "And anything you don't know, you should always ask. You can't be blamed for your ignorance if you ask how to do a job, but if you don't ask about it, and then do it wrong, you *can* be blamed—and punished for it."

"I shall remember that," said Henry, seriously.

"Remember also, as a midshipman you are an apprentice officer," said Robert, "and the best thing you can do is to listen to all the orders the officers give. Then try to find out *why* the order was given. If the mate orders sail taken in, notice whether or not the wind has increased or shifted—understand?"

"Why, yes," said Henry, happily. "That seems like a very simple way to learn how to command a ship."

"Well," said Robert, laughing. "It's the *best* way, but it may not be as simple as it sounds. If it *were* simple, they wouldn't make us stay midshipmen for five years before we can qualify as officers, would they?"

Robert's advice to observe and ask questions did help Henry. Twelve days after leaving Plymouth, he had even learned how longitude was measured.

The captain, one day when both he and Henry were on watch at the same time, seized the opportunity to tell him. "You see, Mr. Wilson," he explained, "there is a town in England named Greenwich, which all seafaring nations have agreed to call 'zero longitude.' Now what we do is this: Along with us on these voyages, we carry two clocks, or chronometers, which are set to show us what time it is in Greenwich. We carry two just in case one fails.

"When we want to know our longitude, we 'shoot the sun,' observing its altitude, and thus find out what time it is where we are. Then, the difference between the time at Greenwich and the time where we are tells us how far we are east or west of Greenwich.

"For instance: We know that the earth travels about a thousand miles in an hour at the equator. Now suppose we were on the equator and shot the sun and found that it was eleven o'clock in the morning. We look at the chronometers and find that it is twelve o'clock noon in Greenwich. It is one hour earlier where we are than it is in Greenwich, so we know that we are about a thousand miles west of Greenwich. That is just an example, of course. We can be much more accurate than that."

After the ship left the Canary Islands, Henry began to practice shooting the sun every time he went on watch. He was a little surprised, about three weeks later, when he shot the sun just after going on watch one day and found that the time where they were was exactly the same as the time shown on the chronometers.

He mentioned this to Philip Benger, the first mate, and Benger explained, "Well, Mr. Wilson, it simply means that if you were a bird and could fly due north from this spot, you would eventually come to Greenwich. We are

13

at zero longitude, some distance due south of Greenwich."

The first mate, some years younger than the captain, was a fine looking man. He had begun his career at sea as a midshipman, so he knew how Henry felt on his first voyage, and he tried to be as helpful as possible.

There was also the old seaman, named Zachariah Allen, who had sailed with Captain Cook.

Allen was about sixty years old, short and slightly stooped. His skin, battered by a lifetime's exposure to wind and salt spray, looked like leather. Encouraged by Benger, he told Henry of Cook's last voyage to the Sandwich Islands. "It was terribly awful. Them Sandwich Island cannibals stabbed him in the back, and I don't doubt that they made quite a feast of him."

"Where were you when Captain Cook was killed?" Henry asked.

"I was in the long boat at the beach there in Karakakooa Bay—the place which Mr. Bligh had discovered for us to drop anchor in—and was waiting for Lieutenant Philips, the Marine officer, to come back, when all the shootin' started," said Allen. "We pulled away from the shore then, but Cap'n Cook, he came down to the edge of the water and waved to us to come back and cease firin'. That's when them cannibals stabbed him in the back. They wouldn't never touch him whilst he was lookin' at 'em."

"Why do you suppose they killed him? Hadn't he treated them fairly?"

"Oh, yes," said Allen. "Cap'n Cook was a very kind man. But you see, sir, them cannibals thought he was a

14

god when he was there the first time. It seems they have a story that hundreds of years ago, a white god sailed to them from the East. After he'd stayed with 'em for a while, he sailed back toward the East, tellin' 'em that he would come back some day. So when Cap'n Cook came, they thought he was their god comin' back to 'em.

"But when we sailed away, and then come back again in a few months, they couldn't understand why a god would come back so soon. That was when they started doubtin' that he *was* a god. And when he started arguin' with 'em—that was when them Marines started shootin'. Then Cap'n Cook tried to stop the shootin', and one of them cannibals stabbed him, and when they seen the blood, they knowed he wasn't no god, so they killed him."

"What did you think of Master Bligh?" asked Benger.

"He is a fine man, sir. Tough as they come, and won't allow nobody to cross him, but a real sailor, sir."

"I know Bligh only by reputation," said the mate. "But I can't say as I like him. He is *too* tough, from what I hear."

"But Master Bligh can handle near any kind of trouble that might come his way, sir, and this new ship he's been given command of—the *Bounty*—will be the best run ship in His Majesty's service. Oh, he keeps a taut ship, sir, and he takes no nonsense from his crew."

By the time the *Antelope* pulled into Cape Town, the mate and Henry were friends. With Robert White, they climbed the hill which is the southernmost tip of Africa, and as they looked out over the city and the dozens of ships lying at its docks, Benger told them of his many voyages to every part of the globe. He had fought with pirates, been captured by them, and escaped from them. But none of his narrow escapes—and there had been many—had made him want to give up his career at sea. It was his home, he said, and though it was sometimes very cruel, it was always beautiful.

After the ship left Cape Town, the winds became weak and on one occasion, the *Antelope* lay becalmed for three days. The ocean was as smooth as glass, and the sails hung limp from the yardarms.

On the morning of their third day in the calm, the captain ordered the long boat lowered and a line strung between it and the ship. The men in the long boat began towing the ship.

Late that afternoon, there was a slight rustle in the sails. The long boat was quickly hauled aboard, and in a few minutes, the sails began filling with wind.

When the long boat had been stowed away, the first mate, who had been in charge, climbed the ladder to the bridge where Captain Wilson and Henry were standing.

"Well, Mr. Benger, luck was with us today," said the captain.

"It was, sir. Only nine hours of rowing before we ran into the wind."

"*Only* nine hours!" said Henry. "That seems like a long enough time to me to be rowing a long boat."

"Aye, Mr. Wilson," said Benger. "It is a long enough time. But once, off the west coast of South America, we rowed day and night for nine *days*."

"Nine days!" gasped Henry. "But couldn't you just

16

have waited for the wind instead of rowing for so long?"

"Not where we were, lad," said Benger. "Southwest of the Galapagos Islands, there is a spot where the winds seldom blow, except for storms. A little storm blew us into the doldrums, and we had to row ourselves out."

Then, turning to Captain Wilson, Benger said, "Sir, if I may offer a suggestion?"

"Of course, Mr. Benger," said the captain.

"Though we did not plan to stop at Batavia, sir, I think that perhaps it would be a good idea. It is taking us a devilishly long time to make the Straits of Sunda, and our water and other supplies—especially limes—are getting very low."

The first mate was right to be worried about the supply of limes, for without them—or fresh vegetables—the crew would certainly begin to suffer from scurvy before they could reach Macao. Captain Cook had discovered, on an earlier voyage, that limes could keep scurvy down if there were no fresh vegetables for the crew to eat, so all English ships had begun to carry a large supply of limes on voyages of any great distance. It was from this practice of carrying limes that the English sailors got the nickname, "Limeys."

Two weeks later, the *Antelope* docked in the port of Batavia on the western tip of the island of Java, and Henry got his first glimpse of life in the tropical islands. In Cape Town, Henry had seen the docks, the English settlement, and the hill that rose just behind the settlement. Here in Batavia he was seeing for the first time how the natives of the islands lived. He was amazed at their odd costumes, and their huts on stilts. The thatched roofs looked familiar to him, for many of the houses in England were roofed with similar material. He was especially surprised to see that everyone traveled by canoe. Even the smallest boys had their own canoes and paddled them swiftly from one place to the next.

Henry got only a glimpse of the jungle which surrounded the town, but he saw enough of it to wonder what sort of strange creatures, both man and beast, might lurk in its mysterious darkness.

"No, Mr. Wilson," said Philip Benger, when Henry asked him. "I have never been into the interior of Java, but I hear that there are head-hunters back there in the mountains, and almost every kind of animal that you ever heard of."

2

Two days after arriving at Java, the *Antelope* pulled out of the harbor at Batavia and set sail on the last leg of her journey to Macao. No more land was seen until, a month later, the coast of China loomed up off the port side of the ship. Two days later, four-and-a-half months after leaving Plymouth, the *Antelope* sailed into Macao.

Before the ship could reach its dock, a small boat came alongside, bearing two officials of the East India Company.

In the captain's cabin, one of them, Mr. Lane, broke bad news: "Captain Browne and the *Gazelle* and all of her crew are missing, Captain Wilson."

"Missing!" exclaimed the captain.

"Yes, I'm afraid so. He was last sighted near the island of Mindoro, in the Philippine group, and he has not been heard from since."

Captain Wilson looked very grave. Alfred Browne and he had grown up together and had gone to sea together as midshipmen.

"He could have easily been delayed," said Mr. Bruce, the other official. "But we don't want to take any chances. We want you to sail to England by way of Cape Horn. On the way you can search for the *Gazelle*."

"Supplies are now waiting for you on the dock," said Mr. Lane. "We will begin loading them immediately, and you should be completely prepared to get under way within a very few days."

Henry did not see very much of China. Like everyone else aboard the *Antelope*, he had to work from early morning until far into the night, carrying supplies onto the ship until she was loaded in record time.

Under ordinary circumstances, the *Antelope* would have stayed in Macao for at least a month, while it was being refitted for the voyage back to England. This time, by the late afternoon of Sunday, July 20, 1783, she was ready to get under way.

Mr. Bruce and Mr. Lane once more appeared on board, and they had someone with them. He was a short, dark-haired man, and he was introduced to Captain Wilson as Thomas Rose.

"Mr. Rose," Mr. Bruce explained to the captain, "will

20

go with you as your interpreter. He is an accomplished linguist and can speak to any foreign ships you may meet. He should be of great help to you in finding Captain Browne."

When Philip Benger came up on the bridge to report that all was ready, the captain introduced him.

"You look familiar to me, Mr. Rose," said the first mate. "Have we sailed together?"

"No, I am sure we have not," said Rose, drawing away from Benger. "I have not taken very many sea voyages, and I am sure that I would remember you if we had sailed on the same vessel."

"Oh," said Benger. "Well, you must resemble someone I have known."

"Yes, I am sure that must be it," said Rose.

Bruce and Lane climbed down to the dock. The lines were cast off, and the *Antelope* drifted slowly out to sea.

The next morning, there was no land to be seen in any direction. The mysterious land of China, which Henry had wanted so badly to see, had disappeared. But when he thought that by the time he arrived back in England, he would have made a complete circumnavigation of the globe, his disappointment faded.

How many other boys his age had been all the way around the world? How many other boys his age had even been around both the Cape of Good Hope and Cape Horn?

"Mr. Wilson!" The voice behind him, saying his name so sharply, made Henry jump.

"Go up to the crow's nest and relieve Duncan," said

21

Captain Wilson, gruffly. "We shall need him on deck to help take in some sail. And I suggest," he added, "that you save your daydreams for your off-duty hours."

"Aye, aye, sir," said Henry, and he dashed for the rope ladder and began the long climb to the top of the mainmast.

Henry had stood watch in the crow's nest before, but never in a rough sea such as they were beginning to encounter now. And as he stood on the little platform and clasped the railing with both hands, the ship was beginning to roll from side to side, like a big dog lying on its back and rolling in a flower bed.

With each roll, Henry would watch the ship seemingly move out from under him and leave him suspended far out over the water. Each time he was sure that the ship was going to roll so far that he would be down to the tops of the whitecaps, but each time it would right itself, and he would be swung out over the other side.

Henry was so fascinated by being swung like an upside-down pendulum that he almost did not hear the faint voice of the captain calling to him.

"Mr. Wilson!" The captain's voice sounded as if it were coming from a great distance. "You are up there to watch for danger, not the rolling of this ship!"

Four hours later, Henry was relieved from his lookout post by Robert White. When he reached the rolling, pitching deck, he felt as if he were standing on firm ground, compared to the swaying he had experienced at the top of the mast.

"You had better go below and eat," said his father. "You may be needed on deck again in the afternoon."

"Aye, aye, sir," said Henry, and he stumbled down the stairs to the galley.

As he went past Mr. Benger's door, Henry heard a loud thump, and then a softer thud. He stopped to listen and heard the sounds repeated. Something must have come loose and was battering against the bulkhead, Henry thought. He opened the door just as Philip Benger rose from his mattress, which was lying on the floor near the wall.

Benger looked around in surprise. A slight smile came to his lips as he saw Henry's puzzled face. "Oh, hello, Henry."

"I heard a noise," Henry explained, "and thought I should see if something had broken loose in here."

"No, nothing's broken loose. I was just practicing my fighting technique—in case we should run into any sort of trouble," said Benger.

"Fighting technique?"

"Yes," said Benger. "It's something I learned in France when I was there. At the time, I considered myself very good with my fists, but a little Frenchman not half my size almost demolished me by using this technique." Then, after a slight pause, he said, "Would you like to learn it? All you have to do is use your feet."

"Feet? How can you fight with your feet?"

"Well, now, look here," said the mate, pointing to an X chalked on the bulkhead. "Just suppose that this X is a man's head. He is getting ready to attack you, so you face him squarely. Then you take a couple of running steps toward him, and when you are about two steps in front of him, you leap into the air, throwing your feet up level

23

with your head. As your body flies through the air toward him, you kick with both feet. Like this." And with that, Benger ran toward the wall, kicked his feet into the air, and turned his body so that it was lying horizontally, with his left side toward the floor. As his body sailed through the air, he doubled his legs up under him and kicked forward with both feet. They hit the X squarely with a tremendous thump. Then he fell to the mattress on the floor.

"Now you try it," he said to Henry, as he picked himself up.

"All right." Henry took aim at the X, ran toward it, and jumped. His feet landed well below it, though, and he stumbled backward onto the mattress.

"If you are afraid of hurting yourself when you fall back, you will never get your feet high enough," said the mate. "Just think of how much worse you might get hurt if you miss your opponent, and he attacks you."

Henry kept trying, but each time his feet dropped down just as he was about to reach the X, and he stumbled backward and fell onto the mattress. Finally, he remembered that he had not eaten his lunch.

"You run on, now, Henry," said Benger. "We'll practice more later, and you'll get it down all right."

But neither Henry nor Philip Benger had any time to practice the new fighting style for a long while. For the next week the weather continued rainy and windy, and all hands were kept busy holding the ship under control.

Though the *Antelope* was not in any danger, she was heavily loaded for her long voyage, and this made her roll more than she ordinarily did.

24

As a result, tons of water poured over her sides. Most of it ran off the decks and back into the sea; much of it spilled down into the ship. All of this, of course, had to be pumped out with the hand pumps. It was back-breaking work, and the men who were put on the pumps did a great deal of grumbling.

One day, when Henry was sweating over the pumps, the mate decided that he needed Henry's sharp eyes up in the crow's nest. He had Henry called up, and ordered one of the seamen, named James Bluitt, to take Henry's place at the pumps.

"Bluitt," said Benger, "go down and man the pumps while Mr. Wilson goes to the crow's nest."

Bluitt scowled and looked at Henry. "You captain's sons allus gits the easy jobs," he growled.

Now Bluitt, while some years older than Henry, had sailed only once before, and his work until now had always been done on deck. He had never been to the crow's nest, or even to a yardarm, since his brawn was more useful in heaving on the deck lines.

"What was that, Bluitt?" said Benger.

"I been noticin'," said Bluitt, "that whenever it comes to hard work, it's us seamen that has to do it. The young captain's son don't have nothin' to do but romp around the riggin' or sit on his backside in the crow's nest."

"Very well," said Benger, glaring at Bluitt. "You go to the crow's nest." Then, turning to Henry, he said, "You may go back to the pumps, Mr. Wilson. We will give Bluitt the rest he so richly deserves."

Bluitt grinned.

"Up with you," said Benger, and Bluitt scrambled up

25

the ladder. He climbed hastily up the first thirty or forty rungs, but then began to go more slowly. By the time he was two-thirds of the way up, he was climbing at a snail's pace, and when he got to within ten feet of the top, he stopped completely and just clung to the ropes.

"Bluitt!" shouted Benger. "Get along up there!"

Bluitt moved up three or four feet, and then he stopped again.

"Get along with you!" shouted Benger again.

"I can't," Bluitt said, his voice floating down weakly to the bridge.

"Bluitt!" shouted Benger angrily. "If you climb down from there now, I'll give you a hundred lashes that you won't likely forget for a long time."

But Bluitt needed no threats to make him stay aloft. His hands and feet were glued to the ladder with fear, and he could not move in either direction. He simply hung there on the ropes, clinging to them with all his strength.

Finally, since Bluitt was completely useless where he was, Benger called for Henry and ordered him to the crow's nest. Henry climbed up the ladder on the other side of the ship and crawled into the crow's nest. For three hours he sat there, with Bluitt clinging to the ropes just a few feet below him. When Henry started to climb down at the end of his watch, Bluitt began pleading with him.

"Please, Mr. Wilson," he said. "I was only jokin'. I didn't really mean what I said. Won't you please help me get down from here?"

Henry looked down into the pitiful face staring up at

him. "Very well," said Henry. "It's really quite simple. Just fix your eyes on the rope in front of you, and don't let yourself look at anything else—then just climb down. Don't look down, whatever you do, or you'll never get back to the deck."

Bluitt silently fixed his gaze on the rope in front of him and started to take the first step down. As he moved his foot, he glanced down at the next rung. When he saw how high above the sea he was, he gasped and grabbed the ropes again tighter than ever.

"I can't! I can't!" he cried.

"I told you not to look down," said Henry angrily. "Now you just do as I said, or you can stay right where you are." And with that, Henry scrambled down the ladder and back to the deck.

"I told him how to get down, but he's too frightened," Henry said to Benger when he reached the bridge.

"He won't come down now until he falls," Benger said, grimly. "And that shouldn't be very long."

Another man was sent up to the crow's nest. After he had been on watch for about an hour, he suddenly shouted, "Look out below! Bluitt's going to fall!"

Everyone on deck looked up, just in time to see the man crumple up and fall backward out into space. Bluitt was on the starboard side of the ship, and just as his strength failed, the ship made a mighty roll to starboard. Bluitt's body hurtled through the air, barely missing the railing of the ship, and hit the water with a resounding splash.

Immediately, the *Antelope* was swung around into the wind to stop her, and a boat was lowered. With direc-

27

tions called to them by the man in the crow's nest, the boat crew soon picked Bluitt out of the water and brought him back to the ship. As he crawled over the railing, frightened and dripping wet, Benger met him.

"You're a lucky man, Bluitt," said Benger. "Just remember, the next time I hear you complaining I shall give you another 'rest' aloft."

The heavy weather kept up for two more days, but the next Sunday—a week from the day the *Antelope* had left Macao—Henry stepped up on deck to find the sea quiet, the sky a beautiful blue, and land visible off the port bow!

Henry ran excitedly to the bridge. "Father—I mean, Captain!" he said. "Is *that* an island?"

The land which they were seeing stretched out along the horizon, on their port side, as far as they could see in both directions, and it was much larger than Henry had expected a South Sea island to be. In his mind, he had pictured the islands as very small dots—as they appeared on the maps—with a few palm trees waving over them.

"Yes," said the captain. "That is Mindoro, one of the Philippines."

"Are we going to land here, sir?" Henry asked.

"No," said the captain. "We are simply going to scout around these islands for a while for any trace of the *Gazelle*."

"Are there cannibals on these islands?" Henry asked.

"I don't know, my boy," said the captain. "But it was on one of these islands that the great Magellan was killed by natives, so we shan't chance going ashore, even though that was a long time ago."

After the short Sunday morning service which was led by the captain, the men were told to keep a sharp eye out for any signs of wreckage, or anything else that might indicate that the *Gazelle* had been in the area. A gold sovereign was promised to the man who spotted any sign that would lead them to the crew of the lost ship.

For a week the *Antelope* sailed among the Philippines, pulling into coves and bays, constantly on the lookout, but without result.

"Mr. Benger," said the captain to the mate finally one day. "We have searched every island on the route that Captain Browne must have taken and have not seen the slightest trace of him. Do you agree that Yap and Ulithi and some of the other islands in the Carolines group would be the next logical place to look?"

"Yes, Captain, I do agree," said Benger.

"Very well, set a course for Yap and get us under way."

For the next few days the weather was calm, and no land was sighted by the *Antelope,* but on Wednesday, the ship ran into a storm, and for three days it was tossed about relentlessly by the raging winds. On Saturday, late in the afternoon, the storm stopped as suddenly as it had begun. The sun came out, just above the horizon. The men were able to open the portholes again and air out their quarters. And Mr. Benger was able to take a sighting. But, by the late evening of Sunday, August 10, 1783, the storm was raging even harder than before.

Suddenly, out of the blackness that encircled the crow's nest, came the bone-chilling cry, *"Breakers! Dead ahead!"*

29

3

The warning had scarcely reached Mr. Benger on the quarter-deck and Captain Wilson in his cabin when there was a grinding jolt which sent everyone sprawling.

The captain scrambled to his feet and ran to the quarter-deck. "What has happened, Mr. Benger?" he shouted through the sound of the wind, rain, and breakers.

"We've hit a reef, Captain. She's pretty badly stove in, sir!"

The captain rushed to the side of the ship and peered

31

down into the darkness. As each wave broke and then receded, he could see the jagged edge of the coral reef jutting out of the water. He could also catch occasional glimpses of the gaping hole in the *Antelope*'s side. Water rushed into the hole, but the ship was hung on the reef and was in no immediate danger of sinking.

The crew assembled in front of the quarter-deck, anxiously waiting for the captain's orders.

"Mr. Benger," ordered the captain, "take men and axes and cut away the masts before their weight pulls the ship over."

"Aye, aye, sir," shouted Benger.

"You there!" called the captain, pointing to one group of sailors. "Go to the galley and bring up as much food and water as you can carry." He pointed to another group. "You men bring the powder and small arms on deck and put them under cover where they won't get wet. The rest of you get the longboat and the pinnace in the water under the lee side of the ship."

Turning to Peter Barker, the second mate, who was now standing beside him, Captain Wilson said, "Mr. Barker, you take charge of the pinnace and hold it alongside until we see how dangerous our position is."

Barker gave a quick nod and ran to help lower the boat into the water. The captain then turned to the third mate. "Mr. Cummin," he said, "relieve Mr. Benger and take charge of cutting away the masts. Tell Mr. Benger to take charge of the longboat."

Captain Wilson then turned to Henry and Robert White, both of whom had been standing impatiently waiting for orders. "You midshipmen, gather the charts, chronometers, compasses, and the rest of the navigation equipment together in the cabin, put them in their cases and bring them up on deck." Then he exclaimed, "Where is Mr. Sharp?"

"I don't know, sir," Robert said. "He came on deck with me just after we ran aground, but I haven't seen him since."

"Well, find him!"

The two boys ran to the midshipmen's quarters to see if Sharp had returned there. They opened the door. Sharp was very busy, packing his personal belongings into his sea bag.

"What are you doing?" Robert asked.

"We're going to sink!" cried Sharp, "and I'm saving my stuff." He glanced around at them and they could see that he was terrified, but not to the extent of forgetting his own comfort.

"You'd better help us get the navigation equipment on deck and into the boats," said Henry. "Your stuff is not going to do *anyone* any good if we have to abandon ship without charts or instruments. Now come on!"

"No!" shouted Sharp, putting his extra shoes into his bag. "I'm not going to let my things sink with this ship!"

Henry and Robert looked at each other and knew that talking was a waste of time. Together they grabbed Sharp and shoved him through the door. Henry picked up a large piece of wood which had fallen down into the passageway when the mainmast had been chopped down. "If you don't come with us, I'm going to brain you," he said, waving the stick in the air menacingly.

Sharp looked at the stick and then at the two boys.

"All right, all right, I'll help," he grumbled, and the three of them made their way aft toward the captain's cabin.

Up on deck, the sailors were still briskly loading the two boats as quickly as the supplies were brought up. Mr. Benger had been directing the loading of the long-boat, and during a lull in the activity, walked back to the quarter-deck, where Captain Wilson was overseeing the entire loading operation.

"Captain Wilson," he asked, "will we abandon ship when the loading is completed?"

"No," said the captain. "We are fairly safe at present. In the morning, we will be able to tell the extent of the damage and whether or not we can save the ship. If we were to put to sea in the small boats in this storm and in the dark, we would be in a very bad position."

"But, sir! In a bright flash of lightning a few moments ago I saw what must be an island to the north of us. We might be able to make that tonight."

"*If* there is land there, Mr. Benger," said the captain, "we *might* be able to make it. But can you say for sure that we won't encounter hostile natives as soon as we set foot on shore?"

"No, sir, of course not."

"Very well, then," said Captain Wilson. "We shall remain on board tonight. The island will still be there in the morning, Mr. Benger."

All through the night the men brought supplies up on the deck. Those considered absolute necessities in case they had to make a long voyage in the small boats were loaded immediately into the long boat and the pinnace. The others were stacked carefully so that they could easily be loaded.

When the first light of dawn broke the darkness, the storm had slackened somewhat. And in a few minutes an island, about four miles to the north of the ship, could be seen. There was another island, much farther, to the east of them.

The captain called the carpenter. "Mr. Polkinghorn," he said, "we will be going ashore soon. While we are gone, I want you to begin building a raft, so that we can remove as much of our supplies as possible in one load if we find the island inhabitable."

"Will we be abandoning the ship for good, sir?" asked the carpenter.

"Not necessarily," said the captain. "If the ship breaks up when the tide goes out, we will have to abandon her, of course. But if she doesn't break up, almost everyone will have to leave anyhow so that we can repair her."

"Aye, aye, sir," said Polkinghorn, and he went to find Richard Jenkins, the carpenter's mate.

"Mr. Benger," called the captain.

"Aye, sir," said the mate, approaching the quarter-deck.

"Mr. Benger, I want you to take the pinnace and as many men as it will hold and go ashore. See if you can find a decent place for us to shelter ourselves. Try to determine if the island is inhabited or not and if there is a source of fresh water."

In less than fifteen minutes, Benger had cast off from the ship and started for shore. The rest of the people aboard the *Antelope*, except for those helping to build the raft, relaxed for the first time since the ship had run aground. James Swift, the cook, had been able to find some biscuits and wine, and these he brought up to the quarter-deck.

"Captain," he said, "the men ain't had nothin' to eat for a long time. Would it be all right if I passed these biscuits and the wine around amongst them?"

The captain did not answer the cook directly. Instead, he went to the rail just above the main deck. "Men," he said, "Mr. Swift has some biscuits and wine which he will pass around to you. You may have a glass of wine before you have your biscuit, in order to get the chill off of you, and you may have another glass of wine to drink with your biscuit. But that is all the intoxicating liquor you may have.

"You have done good work during the past few long hours, and I am not going to have anyone getting drunk and putting all your work to naught. I will have to have your word that you will not drink more than the share that will be given to you."

The sailors shouted their approval.

While the men were having their breakfast, Captain Wilson and his boatswain, William Harvey, went to the side of the ship to see if they could tell how much damage had been done.

"Do you think she'll slip off of the reef when the tide goes out, Mr. Harvey?" asked the captain.

"It's hard to tell, Captain," said Harvey. "She may slip off, but on the other hand she may hang right where she is. The way she's leaning toward the reef, I think she'll hang, but it is terribly hard to judge."

"It depends pretty largely on how steep this outer face of the reef is," said the captain. "With the water still covering it, it's difficult to tell."

Suddenly, from the forward end of the ship, came a terrified scream. It was followed immediately by a shout from Robert White, "Man overboard!"

Everyone jumped up and ran to the side of the ship. In the water, tangled in the shroud lines of the foremast, was Henry, fighting desperately to keep from being tugged under the water. In an instant, Robert White stripped off his jacket, snatched a knife from a sailor, and jumped into the water. He began hacking furiously at the ropes, but he was having trouble keeping Henry above water and cutting the ropes at the same time.

"Throw him a line!" he shouted. "Throw him a line!"

When one of the sailors did, Robert got the ropes cut quickly. He helped Henry to the side of the ship, where both of them were pulled aboard.

"What were you doing?" said the captain, angrily, as Henry crawled onto the deck. "Can't you keep yourself from falling overboard?"

"I was trying to cut the foremast loose, Captain," said Henry excitedly. "All of the lines holding it were not cut and it's pounding into the ship every time a wave breaks."

The captain and the others looked over the side. With every wave, the broken end of the mast was battering against the side of the ship. It was a wonder that it had

37

not already knocked another hole in the bottom of the ship.

"Cut those lines!" shouted the captain. A sailor immediately jumped up on the railing and hacked the ropes in two with an axe.

"You were trying to do the right thing, Henry, but you should not put yourself in such a dangerous position unless someone is with you."

"Yes," said Robert. "You're lucky I happened by just when I did. With all the noise of the breakers, we might not have heard you call for help."

"Well," said the captain, "I think Mr. Wilson will not take any more foolish chances. Now you two get below and change into some dry clothes if you have any."

At about noon, the pinnace returned to the ship and Benger came aboard. "We have found a very nice harbor, Captain. It's small, but it is protected from the wind. There is a good supply of fresh water from a spring not far from the beach, and I think it will make an ideal place for us to stay."

"Any signs of life?" asked the captain.

"None whatever," said Benger. "We didn't get a chance to explore the entire island—I think it is three or four miles long. I left five of the men to clear a spot of ground where we can put up shelters, and I told them that most of us would probably come ashore this afternoon."

"Excellent!" said the captain happily. "We will finish loading the raft which Mr. Polkinghorn has just completed and get everyone ashore. Then we can return to the ship in the morning and try to patch her up."

38

"What do you think our chances are of repairing her and getting away from here, Captain?" asked Benger in a low voice.

Captain Wilson lowered his voice, too. "If the *Antelope* will hold together for four or five days, I think we can get her fixed up well enough to get her back to Macao, if we keep the pumps going around the clock," he said. "If she breaks up before then, we will have to stay on that island until another ship comes by and picks us up."

Benger grinned wryly. "Since we are far south of the routes traveled by any ships, and since this island does not even exist so far as the rest of the world knows, we should probably have to wait quite a long time for *that*, sir," he said.

By midafternoon, everyone was ready to leave the ship. The two boats were pulled alongside and the men climbed aboard, taking up their oars. The captain was the last man to step off the *Antelope*; under his arm he carried the ship's flag.

"Well, old girl," said the captain, looking back at his ship, "I hope you can keep your chin above water."

It was just beginning to get dark when the two boats and the raft, stacked with food, pulled into the harbor. The five men on shore were shouting with joy. They had not been able to see the ship or the boats because of the rain which had started again, and had begun to think that they were the only ones still left alive.

In order to keep busy, they had not only cleared a large section of ground, but had erected a tent as well. This they had made out of a sail, and it provided a very nice

39

shelter for the captain and the other officers. The rest of the men took spots of their own choosing and made small, individual shelters of palm leaves or pieces of sail.

After the men were settled, the captain called them all together. "We will stand watches the same as on board ship," he said. "Keep an especially sharp lookout; we can not be certain that the island is uninhabited. Because of this, and in accordance with maritime law, I warn you that any man caught asleep while on guard will be shot. Mr. Benger will show those on guard where their posts are. Goodnight."

"Goodnight, Captain." The men turned in for the first real rest they had had in thirty-six hours.

4

The sun shone brightly just above the horizon as the crew of the *Antelope* awoke. The water in the lagoon between the island and the reef which surrounded it was softly rolling and of the deepest blue imaginable.

While the cook was preparing breakfast, the captain called a meeting before the tent. "As you can see, men," he said, "the *Antelope* is still lodged on the reef. But every movement of the tide is a threat to her safety and ours. Today, Mr. Polkinghorn, Mr. Jenkins, Mr. Benger, and half the crew will go out to the reef with me to begin the repairs. The rest of you will stay on the island and make a more comfortable encampment for all of us. Mr. Barker, you and Mr. Cummins will be in charge ashore."

He looked around at the men gathered before him. They looked eager to do anything and everything he might suggest which would get them safely back to civilization.

"I see that breakfast is ready, now," said the captain, glancing across the clearing toward the cook. "So eat hearty, men. There is hard work ahead of us."

While the men were lining up, the captain called Richard Sharp and Robert White over. "Mr. Sharp, you and Mr. White serve breakfast to the men while the cook prepares some food to take with us out to the reef."

"Aye, aye, sir," said White.

Sharp, however, did not move. "Why can't some of the sailors serve the food?"

Captain Wilson stared at him, a frown creasing his forehead. "What do you mean, Mr. Sharp?"

"Mr. White and I are supposed to be learning how to be ship's officers, sir," said Sharp, "not how to wait on the common seamen's table."

Captain Wilson glared at Sharp for a few moments. "You are quite right, Mr. Sharp," he said finally. "You did come aboard the *Antelope* to learn how to be an officer."

Sharp smiled.

"Among the many things which a man must learn in order to become a ship's officer, Mr. Sharp, are these," continued the captain. "First, he must learn to take orders as well as give them. And second, he must be willing and able, in times of emergency or danger, to do any job which will further the common good of his ship and his crew.

"I had intended to rotate the job of cook's helper among all of the crew, so that no one would have to spend more than one day as server or dishwasher every two weeks, but I shall give you that job permanently, in order that your education as an officer will not be neglected."

With that, Captain Wilson turned on his heel and went toward the longboat. Richard Sharp, his face red with embarrassment, stood for a moment staring after the captain, then he slowly turned and walked over to the waiting men.

On the *Antelope*, later on in the morning, the crew set about clearing the rubble from the deck while the captain, the carpenter and his helper, and Mr. Benger examined the damaged section of the ship.

"Well, sir," said the carpenter, after they had looked the situation over, "as you can see, she has a pretty large hole in her side, and she's hanging by that big piece of coral that juts out from the reef."

"Yes, I can see that much, Mr. Polkinghorn," said the captain. "Can we get her loose from the coral?"

"I think we could pry her loose, Captain," said the carpenter, "but that rock is all that's holding her up. She'd sink for sure if she broke loose."

"Her bottom is resting on the face of the reef when the tide is out, though," said Captain Wilson. "Perhaps we could pry her loose or cut her loose at low tide, and slip a sail around her outside to keep her from sinking when the tide comes in. Then we could pump her dry and repair her from the inside."

"Aye, sir," said the carpenter. "The pressure of the water would hold a sail against the hole and keep a great deal of water from coming in while we blocked up the hole permanently from the inside. It would take fast work, though, to get the job done before the tide came back in."

"Captain," said Mr. Benger, "I've been in a similar situation and would like to tell you how we solved the problem then."

"I'm willing to listen to any reasonable suggestions Mr. Benger."

"When the *John Smythe* ran upon a rock off the coast of Spain some years ago," said Benger, "we simply built a water-tight room inside the ship. It was built completely around the hole in the side and the rock that made the hole. Then we pumped her out and were able to sail on to France before having the hole repaired."

"Mr. Polkinghorn," said Captain Wilson. "Could we do the same?"

"No, sir," said the carpenter. "I've heard about the *John Smythe*, and her situation was a little different from ours. She went straight onto that rock and was just punctured, so to speak, whereas we come down on top of this here reef and was slashed open. The water's too deep in the compartment where the slash is for us to be able to build a room around the hole. No, sir, we're just going to have to chop her loose and get a sail around her to keep the water out."

"Very well, then," said the captain. "We can't work in the dark, so we will have to wait for a low morning tide."

"Aye, sir," said the carpenter. "I don't think she'll slip

off her perch unless too many people comes aboard and weights her down on the seaward side. But there ain't no danger of that, because them that cuts her loose and holds her to keep her from slipping can stand on the reef at low tide. The water's only about knee-deep then."

"All right," said the captain. "Then here is our procedure: In the morning, just before dawn, we will leave the island. As many men as can do so safely will come aboard the ship and tie ropes to one edge of a sail. The other ends of the ropes will be slipped under the ship and will be held by men on the other side of the deck. The other edge of the sail will be fastened to the deck railing, and the sail will be lowered until it is just above the hole. Then the men on the reef will chop through the side of the ship above the piece of coral. When the ship slips off the coral, the men on the seaward side of the deck will pull on their end of the ropes, pulling the sail tight over the hole. The pumps will be started then, and we hope that she'll be dry enough to float by the time the tide comes back in. Does that meet with your approval, gentlemen?"

"Aye, sir," said the carpenter, and Mr. Benger nodded his head in agreement.

Captain Wilson explained what they hoped to do to the crew on the deck of the *Antelope*. Then, since the sun was almost directly overhead, Mr. Benger distributed the biscuits, dried meat, and water, and everyone sat down on the deck to enjoy his midday meal. As soon as the meal was over, the men returned to work.

In order to lighten the load on the ship, many of the items which had been left behind on the first trip were loaded into the longboat. The small cannons, with their powder and ammunition, were removed. A number of the water kegs, which had been left behind because fresh water was available on the island, were loaded into the boat. And most of the personal belongings of the men were saved—even those which Richard Sharp had been so anxious to rescue.

When the long boat was loaded with all it could carry, everyone clambered aboard. The water of the lagoon was clear and smooth and they made shore well before sundown.

Quite a change had taken place in the clearing. It had been swept clean of rocks, driftwood, and broken shells, and three more tents had been put up. A dutch oven and fire pit had been built for the cook, and a flagpole had even been raised.

After Captain Wilson had congratulated the men on the excellent job they had done ashore, Tom Dulton, Captain Wilson's old steward, approached the captain. "Cap'n, sir," he said. "We've raised a flagpole, but we thought it should be you, sir, who should place our glorious flag upon it."

Captain Wilson placed the flag on the pole and then turned to face the men. "In the name of His Gracious Majesty, George III, King of Great Britain, I claim this island and all other islands in its distinct group for the British Crown."

The men cheered. The captain quieted them down and explained the plan to save the *Antelope* from the reef. Then he directed Mr. Benger to determine the location of the island, so that they could record the claim and bury it beneath a British flag when they left the island.

On the way to his tent, Captain Wilson was stopped by Thomas Rose.

"Captain, I wonder if I might have a few words with you."

"Yes, Mr. Rose," said the captain. "Won't you step into my quarters?"

The two men sat on packing cases. Rose leaned forward, at the same time drawing something from the pocket of his coat.

"Captain, do you know what these are?"

Captain Wilson looked at the objects in Rose's outstretched hand. "Why, of course," he said. "They are fish bones. Why?"

"Today I went to the spring for water, and climbed the hill which rises behind the spring, to see what I could see. That's where I found these," Rose said, pointing to the fish bones.

"On top of the hill?" asked the captain, taking the bones in his hand to examine them more closely. "That is an odd place for fish bones to be."

"Exactly, sir," said Rose. "They were put there by an animal—or by humans. How else could they get there? And I might add, Captain, that none of *us* have caught any fish."

5

Thomas Rose assured the captain as he left the tent that he would not say anything to the crew about his discovery.

Captain Wilson remained for a few moments in deep thought. Then he walked to the opening in the tent. "Mr. Benger," he called. "Will you step in here, please?"

"Yes, sir?" said Benger as he ducked under the flap and into the tent. Then, seeing the worried look on Captain Wilson's face, he asked, "Is anything wrong, Captain?"

"Yes," said the captain, picking up the bones. "These."

Benger looked at the bones in the captain's hand. "Fish bones?" he said, looking at the captain quizzically.

"Mr. Rose found them on the hill overlooking the spring."

"Maybe some of the men . . ."

"No," interrupted the captain. "There has been no fishing by any of the crew. It means that the island is inhabited by humans. If it had been an animal, it would have either eaten the bones, too, or it would have broken them up getting the meat off. It wouldn't have stripped the meat off the bones so cleanly, anyhow."

"Yes, I suppose you are right," said Benger.

"I've decided I should tell the men, Benger. They have every right to know the danger they're in."

"I agree with you completely, sir. Will you tell them now?"

The captain nodded.

Benger ducked through the opening and called the men around the campfire.

As the captain began speaking to his crew, looks of fright appeared on their faces.

"We have not seen any of the natives yet," continued the captain, "so we don't know exactly what to expect of them. For all we know, they may be quite friendly."

"Not bloody likely," said one of the crew members, aloud. "They're cannibals, *I'll* wager."

"All right," said the captain. "Let us remain calm and try to see what our situation really is."

The mumbling of the crew stopped, and all of the men focused their attention on the captain.

"We do not know that the natives are even aware of

our presence on their island," he said. "We are probably in no immediate danger. Now, in the morning some of you will have to stay on the island and make things ready so that we can depart quickly if we have to.

"As soon as the ship is afloat, some of us will come back to the island for the remainder of the supplies and equipment. We should be able, even with only the sail patching the hole, to get some distance out to sea tomorrow night. We can repair the ship more permanently at sea. Are there any questions?"

"Yes, sir," said one of the sailors. "What will we do if we are attacked before morning?"

"There is little danger of that," said Captain Wilson. "Natives on the other islands have always been reluctant to fight at night. If they should attack, though, we have our three cannon and our small arms. Any more questions?"

There was no answer, so the captain turned to Benger. "Mr. Benger," he said, "double the watch tonight and keep the cannon loaded and manned." Then he turned and went back to the tent.

There was not much sleep among the crew of the *Antelope* that night. All of the men felt that their one chance for seeing home again lay in getting the ship afloat before their presence on the island was discovered. When Benger made the rounds just before dawn the next morning to awaken the men, most of them were awake already and anxious to get about their business.

By the time the first sign of day began to appear in the east, breakfast had been eaten and the men were at their stations, ready to shove the boat into the lagoon and begin the trip to the reef. Suddenly, Zachariah Allen, the man who had been with Captain Cook on his ill-fated voyage, and who was now standing at the prow of the longboat, shouted, "Captain! Look!"

All eyes strained in the direction in which the old man was pointing. There, just coming into view from behind the point of land west of the cove, were two canoes with three natives in each. They were rowing straight for the *Antelope*.

"Quickly!" shouted Captain Wilson. "Back to the camp. Mr. Benger, you and Mr. Barker and Mr. Cummins issue arms and ammunition to everyone. Mr. Blanch, man the cannon."

John Blanch, the ship's gunner, picked the men for his gun crews and ripped the canvas covers from the three small cannon. The three mates gave each man a rifle, a handful of balls, and a flask of powder. Then the captain called the men around him in the center of the clearing. He looked out to sea in the direction of the two canoes, which were still moving toward the *Antelope*, and then turned to the men.

"Men," he said, "find yourselves good cover and form a semi-circle around the camp. Keep a sharp eye inland and don't concern yourselves with the two canoes out there. There aren't enough men in them to bother us, and if they are trying to distract our attention seaward, we will have a small surprise for them. To your posts, now! And fire at anything that moves!"

The men ran quickly to strategic points, hiding themselves behind trees, boulders, and anything else that would give them protection from the spears and arrows which they expected to see flying toward them at any moment.

Captain Wilson and Mr. Benger stood back-to-back in the center of the clearing, both of them with pistols in each hand. While the captain kept watch toward the forest and hills inland from the camp, Benger scanned the seaward approach to the island.

After they had been standing in silence for a few minutes, Benger spoke over his shoulder to the captain. "See anything, Captain?" he asked.

"Not a movement," said Captain Wilson without turning his head. "What's going on out there?"

"Nothing," answered Benger. "The two canoes will reach the *Antelope* soon."

"I suppose they will steal everything that is lying loose," said the captain.

"Probably will," said Benger.

"Where is your glass?" the captain asked. "Were you able to save it?"

"Yes, sir," said Benger. "It's in the tent."

"Good," said the captain. "Get it, and if they go aboard, try to see what they are doing."

Without taking the time to reply, Benger ran to the officers' tent, dug his telescope out of his sea bag, and returned. He focused the glass on the canoes. "They've reached the ship now, Captain," he said.

"What are they doing?"

"They're looking her over," answered the mate. "They're looking at the hole in her side. . . . Now one of them is climbing up her side, sir. He's on deck."

"Can you tell what they look like?" asked the captain.

"No, sir," said Benger. "I can just barely distinguish hands and arms, and though they appear to be naked, I couldn't say for sure. Now the rest of them are going aboard, Captain."

"All of them?" asked Captain Wilson.

"No," said Benger. "One is staying behind to keep charge of the canoes."

"Be sure that no other canoes slip up on us while you are watching the *Antelope*, Mr. Benger," said the captain.

"Aye, aye, sir," said Benger. He took the glass away from his eye and scoured the part of the lagoon that he could not see while looking through the telescope. Then he put the telescope to his eye again and began once more to watch the activity aboard the ship.

"Can you tell what they are doing now, Mr. Benger?" the captain asked, after a few more minutes had gone by.

"Yes," said Benger. "It looks as if they are putting some things into the canoes."

"All of our tools, probably," said the captain.

"And now it looks as if they are leaving. Yes, they're coming over the side now and getting into the canoes."

"Hm," said the captain, thoughtfully. "Could you tell whether or not they ever watched us to see what our disposition was?"

"No, sir," said Benger. "I don't remember their looking in this direction while they were paddling out to the ship, and they certainly couldn't have seen much from her deck."

"Well," said the captain. "Even without seeing us,

54

they know that we are here now. They found no bodies on the ship, so they can guess that we made it ashore all right. As it is, the rest of the natives probably won't know we're here until those fellows in the canoes get back where they came from and tell them."

"How long do you think that might be?" asked Benger.

"Well, their village—if they have one—must be some distance from here, or we would have known about it long ago," said the captain. "When they get back to it, they will have to explain what they have found to the others. Then they will probably have to hold a council to decide what they are going to do."

He paused and thought for a few moments. "Then, of course," he added, "they will have to find out exactly where we are. So, I should think that we could expect to see some scouts this afternoon late, but I don't think they can mount an attack until tomorrow morning."

"We have a few hours for making preparations, then," said Benger.

"Yes," said the captain. "And here is what we had better do. Keep half of the men on guard; have the other half chop down some of the nearby trees. We will cut these into six-foot lengths and build a barricade around the camp. Start with the seaward side first, as that is our most vulnerable spot, then continue it around the sides of the camp. If we have time—which we probably won't —we can extend the fence around below the foot of the hill. I think, though, that we are at a safe distance from the hill and don't have to worry too much about being fired upon from there with their spears."

"Aye, aye, sir."

55

The wood of the trees was so soft that the chopping went much more quickly than had been expected, and by midafternoon the seaward side of the barricade was finished. The two arms which were to protect the camp from approach along the beach were well under way, and the second shift of men were still working feverishly.

Tension was beginning to mount. When would the attack come? Would it be before dark? Would it be that night, even though the South Sea island natives were known to prefer fighting in daylight?

The minutes dragged by and became an hour. Then another hour went by, ever so slowly, and at long last darkness crept over the island. Captain Wilson decided to keep half the crew on watch at a time during the night. Mr. Benger set the first watch, and Mr. Swift and Mr. Sharp brought food after everyone was settled in his place.

The captain, turning toward his tent, found Henry at his side. "Henry, my boy," said the captain, "where have you been all day?"

"Well, sir," said Henry, "Mr. Benger gave me a gun this morning when the natives were sighted, and I found a good place behind a tree over near the foot of the hill. I was there all day until this afternoon, when I went out to help chop the trees."

"Why you must be extremely tired, then," said the captain. "Come to the tent with me and we'll have our meal together." He put his arm around his son's shoulders and they walked to the tent.

"Are you frightened, Henry?" the captain asked.

"Oh, no, sir. I think you are handling the situation very well."

"Really?" said the captain. "Thank you, my boy."

"Zachariah Allen says that he would as soon be with you in this kind of situation as with Captain Cook," said Henry.

"Well, that's very kind of Mr. Allen," said Captain Wilson. "And what might the other men have to say?"

"I don't know, sir," said Henry. "But Mr. Allen was telling me today how Captain Cook always tried to approach the natives in a friendly manner. Mr. Allen says that the worst thing about most explorers is that they always assume that the natives are unfriendly, so they shoot the natives as soon as they see them. Then they wonder why all of the natives are unfriendly. But we're going to try to make friends of the natives first, aren't we, Father?"

"My boy," said Captain Wilson, "it's true that most of the explorers have killed natives first and then condemned them for being warlike when they fought back. But you must remember that Captain Cook was killed by some of the very natives he had befriended."

"I know, Father," said Henry. "But if we showed these natives that we intended them no harm why wouldn't they be friendly to us in turn? They have no reason to hurt us if we don't hurt them first."

"Who can say what ideas go through the minds of savages?" the captain said. "It is quite possible these may be friendly, but if we try to be friendly with them and *then* find out that they are cannibals, it will be too late."

The next morning Captain Wilson was awakened by Mr. Benger, and together they aroused the rest of the men. As they paused to shake each sleeping figure, the captain would say, "Keep this place and man the wall with your gun. Keep a sharp eye out for any movement. They should be coming soon."

In only a matter of minutes there was hardly a space along the wall from which a gun did not protrude. Then everyone sat quietly and waited.

The sun had just cleared the horizon when one of the men turned from the wall nearest the sea and ran across the clearing to the captain. At the same time, a whisper raced like wildfire around the wall, from one man to the next. "Here they come!"

6

All heads turned toward the seaward side of the enclosure, the direction in which the natives had been
sighted. There, in full view of the camp, was a large
flotilla of canoes.

"How many do you make them to be, Mr. Benger?"
asked the captain.

"About fifty canoes, sir," said Benger. "And with four
men in each canoe, that would be two hundred natives—
about six to one in their favor."

"Yes," said Captain Wilson. "There may be a lot more

of them over the hill, waiting to attack us. Pass the word to keep a close lookout inland."

"Aye, aye, sir," said Benger.

When the mate returned to the captain, he had his telescope under his arm. "I thought you might like to use this, Captain," he said.

"Thank you," said the captain, taking the glass and focusing it on the canoes. "It looks as if the natives who went out to the ship yesterday have all of their friends interested. They are headed straight for the *Antelope*."

Benger smiled at the captain's grim humor, and then, for over an hour, there was silence as the men watched the canoes approach the ship. Finally, seeing the canoes had reached the reef, Benger spoke to the captain.

"Can you see what they are doing now, Captain?" he asked.

Captain Wilson continued to squint through the glass. "Yes," he said. "They're all wading around on the reef except for one man in each canoe." He paused for a few moments, and then suddenly his whole body seemed to stiffen. "My God!" he exclaimed.

"What is it, Captain?" Benger asked excitedly. "What are they doing?"

"The bloody beggars!" said the captain, angrily. "They're all climbing up her sides." He turned away from the telescope quickly. "Mr. Polkinghorn!" he shouted.

The carpenter ran rapidly from his position along the wall to where the captain was standing. "Aye, sir?" he asked.

The captain handed him the glass.

"They're climbing aboard," said the carpenter.

"Do you think their weight will break her loose from the reef?"

"I'd hate to wager on it either way, Captain," said Polkinghorn, shaking his head. "If it don't, the only reason will be that her bottom's resting on the reef and supporting all the weight. If they stay on her until the tide comes in, though, nothing can save her. With all that weight on her top deck, and nothing under her to support it, she'll roll right off'n that rock she's hanging onto and down she'll go."

"Then I guess there's nothing we can do but wait and pray that they get off before the tide comes in," said the captain. "That will be in about an hour from now, Mr. Benger?"

"Yes, sir," said Benger. "Certainly no more than that."

Henry, who was stationed nearby, had been listening to this discussion. Slowly, with a concerned expression on his face, he walked up to his father. "Captain," he said, "may I offer a suggestion?"

The captain turned, surprised, and said, "Why, yes, Hen . . . er . . . Mr. Wilson."

"Well, sir," said Henry, "maybe if we fired at them with the cannon, they would leave the ship."

The captain turned quickly to Benger. "What do you think, Mr. Benger?" he asked.

"They are out of range, sir," said Benger, "but we could loft a ball fairly close to them."

"Yes," said the captain. "We could almost surely frighten them off, even though we can't actually reach them with our shot. Of course, if they don't know we're

61

here now, they would as soon as we fired the cannon, and they might attack us.

"On the other hand," he said, thinking aloud, "we can't leave the island without a ship, whether they know we are here or not." Then, turning to Benger again, he said, "Mr. Benger, tell the gunner to put a ball as close to those canoes as he can get one."

"Aye, aye, sir."

Captain Wilson turned to Henry and placed his hand on the boy's shoulder. "Thank you, Henry," he said. "Sometimes we older people try to think up complicated ways of solving our problems, while a younger mind can still see clearly the simplest solution."

"I hope it works," said Henry, a little embarrassed.

"Ready, sir," said the gunner, from beside the cannon.

The captain walked over behind the gun and saw that it was aimed for the center of the large group of canoes. He stepped back to give the gunner room to apply his torch. "Ready? *Fire!*"

There was an ear-shattering explosion and all faces turned seaward. A geyser of water shot into the air from a spot about two-thirds of the way to the *Antelope,* and as the spray fell back into the lagoon, the captain called to Mr. Benger, "Did it have any effect on them, Mr. Benger?"

Benger jerked the telescope away from his eye. "They're tumbling all over each other trying to get off the ship," he shouted gleefully. At this news, the men in the enclosure gave a cheer, which quickly died at the ominous sound of a dull rumbling noise.

"She's broken loose!" Mr. Benger cried. "She's sinking!"

As they stood there watching, the *Antelope* rolled slowly over on its side and, with a loud hiss, slipped below the waves of the incoming tide.

When the last trace of the ship had disappeared beneath the foaming breakers, leaving about a hundred of the natives splashing wildly in the water, Captain Wilson was the first to come out of the state of shock.

"Back to your posts!" he shouted.

He watched the men return to their positions along the wall, and then walked back to Benger, who was still looking through his glass.

"They're getting back into their canoes, sir," said the mate. "I can't tell whether any of them were trapped aboard the ship or not."

Captain Wilson heard a noise and turned to find his son standing there, his eyes filled with tears. "It's all my fault," said the boy.

"Why, no, Henry," said the captain. "It isn't your fault at all."

"If I hadn't suggested that we fire the cannon at them, they wouldn't have made the ship sink!"

Captain Wilson put an arm around his son's shoulders and said, "Come to the tent with me and let's get a drink of water."

Inside the tent, the captain again began to talk. "My boy," he said, "if we ever get back to civilization, you will find as you grow older that there are many times in a man's life when he faces a dilemma. There will be times when you will have to decide which of two courses of action you are going to take. One of them may be just as disagreeable or dangerous as the other.

"At such times, you will have to keep calm and consider your problem carefully without wasting time. Then, once you've decided which one you are going to do, do it and do it to the best of your ability. Most important, though, is not to change your mind once you've started, unless the circumstances which created your problem change and cast a completely different light on your situation. That is a pitfall you must learn to avoid."

The captain placed his hand on his son's arm. "Let me explain it this way," he said. "Once there were two brothers who owned a mule, and this mule was standing in the field one day while one of the brothers unloaded a cartload of hay nearby. The mule turned to go and eat the hay, but at that very moment the other brother unloaded a cartload of oats on the other side of the mule.

"Well, the mule looked at the oats and then he looked at the hay, and then he turned away from the hay and started to go and eat the oats. On the way, though, he changed his mind and decided that he liked hay better, so he turned back toward the mound of hay. Just as he reached it, he remembered that he didn't get oats very often, so he turned back toward the mound of oats. But he still couldn't make up his mind, so he sat down between the two mounds and looked from one to the other, trying to choose between them.

"The longer he thought about his problem, the harder it became to decide, until finally, sitting there in the midst of enough food to keep him alive for a month, he starved to death." The captain paused and looked into his son's eyes. "Do you understand what I've been trying to tell you, Henry?" he asked.

Henry smiled at his father. "Yes, sir, I do understand," he said. "And I'll try to remember from now on."

"Good!" said the captain, slapping Henry on the shoulder. "Now let's think no more about what *might* have happened, *if* we hadn't done what we *have already* done."

"Aye, aye, sir," said Henry, and together they walked back to their places along the wall.

All day long the men lay waiting for the attack. Darkness fell, and a double watch was kept through the night, but not a sign of the island's inhabitants was seen. When the sun rose the next morning, Captain Wilson called Mr. Benger to him.

"It is my opinion, Mr. Benger," he said, "that our presence on the island was not known until we fired the cannon yesterday. Even though they had found the ship earlier, it is quite possible that the natives did not know that it was run by men. If they have never seen such an object as our ship before—and I am sure they have not, since the island was undiscovered until we came— they would actually have no reason to expect humans to be aboard the ship. Do you agree?"

"Yes, sir," said Benger. "If they had seen the ship sailing, they might have expected to find people aboard, but just seeing it lying on the reef like that, they probably didn't have any idea of what it was."

"If we are right, then," said the captain, "it explains why we haven't been attacked as yet. Today we can expect to see the scouts we thought we would see a few days ago. The attack should follow the appearance of the scouts by a few hours at the most, don't you think?"

65

"Yes, sir," said Benger. "I quite agree."

"Then tell the men to keep a sharp eye out," said Captain Wilson. "We do not want the scouts to observe our strength without our knowing about it."

"On second thought, sir," said Benger, "do you think they will take the trouble to find out how many of us there are before they attack? They already know *where* we are."

"Yes," said the captain. "I have never heard of any South Sea natives attacking a superior force, so I feel certain that they will scout us first."

The morning dragged by slowly and finally it was lunch time. The captain took his food to the tent and sat down on the ground just outside, his legs crossed under him. He had been there only a few moments when Zachariah Allen stepped up to him, plate in hand.

"Cap-tin," he said. "I wonder if I might have a word with ye?"

"Why, of course, Allen," said the captain. "Won't you sit down?"

"Thank ye kindly, sir," said Allen, his old bones creaking as he lowered himself slowly to the sand near the captain.

"Now, what can I do for you?" the captain asked as soon as the old man was settled.

"Well, sir," said Allen. "It ain't my place to approve or disapprove of the captin's plans. But it does seem to me, sir, that now the ship's gone we're in a very tedious position."

"Yes, that's quite true," said the captain, amused by Allen's use of the word "tedious."

"Now, sir," said Allen. "If anyone was of a mind to ask me, I'd say that, considerin' our position and all, maybe we should try to make a friendly-like approach to them natives. I've seen Cap'n Cook walk right up to natives he'd never seen before, with a big smile on his face, and make friends with them in no more'n a quarter hour, and then we didn't have no trouble with 'em. Oh, there might be a little stealin', but Cap'n Cook, he'd just tell the king that some of the natives was misbehavin', and the king would punish 'em and make 'em stay away from us after that."

"Yes," said the captain. "But some of those 'friendly' natives finally killed Captain Cook."

"Aye, sir, that's true," said Allen. "But all in all, his friendly approach got him a lot farther along with the natives than all the killin' and butcherin' them others did got them. And we do have one advantage Cap'n Cook didn't have when he first come out here, and that's a interpreter."

"You mean Mr. Rose?" asked the captain, surprised.

"Yes, sir," said Allen.

"I thought Mr. Rose only understood European languages, and possibly Chinese."

"No, sir," said Allen. "He says he learned the island language from a native that was picked up by a ship he was on some years ago, and you know Cap'n Cook discovered that the languages on most of the islands is very like each other, so maybe Mr. Rose would be able to talk to these here natives. He could explain that we

don't mean no harm to no one, and then we wouldn't
have to endanger ourselves by killin' some of them and
makin' the rest of them mad."

"Yes," said the captain. "If Mr. Rose *can* communicate
with them, it might be helpful. At any rate, we'll hope
that we get the opportunity to try out Mr. Rose's lin-
guistic ability before we have to try our marksmanship.
I promise you, Allen, that I will do my best to give Rose
his chance. Does that ease your mind?"

"Aye, sir, it does that," said Allen.

Shortly after lunch, the captain walked around inside
the enclosure until he found Thomas Rose. "Mr. Rose,"
he said. "Do you think that you would be able to talk to
the natives on this island?"

"Perhaps, Captain," said Rose. "It's impossible to say
yet whether these natives speak the same language I do
or a dialect of it."

"I understand," said Captain Wilson. "If it is at all
possible, though, I wish to establish friendly relations
with these natives, and should like you to be available
immediately to talk to any we happen to sight."

"Captain! Look!"

The captain and Rose spun around. About a hundred
paces down the beach stood a man, spear in hand, looking directly at the camp. "Speak to him! Quickly!" whispered the captain to Rose.

"*Amuno! Amuno!*" Rose called to the figure, but as
soon as the sound reached him, the native turned quickly
and fled into the forest.

"What did you say to him?" asked the captain.

"I simply invited him to come into our 'house.'"

"Do you think he understood?" asked the captain.

"I don't know, Captain," said Rose. "But I shall try to find out." And with that, he suddenly ran out of the enclosure and down the beach after the native.

"Come back, Rose!" shouted Captain Wilson. "Don't be an idiot! Come back!"

But Rose ran on into the forest.

For the rest of the afternoon, hardly a word was spoken inside the enclosure. Most of the men were wondering what fate Rose had met.

Shortly before dark—and much to everyone's surprise— Rose strode out of the jungle and onto the beach a few yards west of the enclosure.

"Thank God you're safe," said the captain, when Rose entered inside the wall. "Where have you been?"

"I've been trailing that native. I almost caught up with him two or three times," said Rose, "but each time I lost his trail, and by the time I got back on it again, he had gained on me. So I finally lost him altogether."

"Well, that was a foolish thing to do, Mr. Rose," said the captain. "You might have been killed." He turned to the men. "Remember this, all of you. No one is to leave this enclosure alone. Mr. Benger, set the night watches."

Neither Henry, nor Robert White, nor Benger were on watch in the early part of the evening. They were all three sitting with their backs against the wall, looking at the fire some yards away and talking.

Finally, Robert White asked Benger a question he had been wanting to ask him for a long, long time. "Mr.

69

Benger, you were captured by pirates once, weren't you? Would you mind telling us about it?"

Benger hesitated, and Henry added his plea, "Please, Mr. Benger."

"Well, all right," said Benger. Then he told his story: "It was almost fifteen years ago—I wasn't much older than you lads when it happened. My ship was attacked by a pirate ship some miles west of Gibraltar, and though we put up a good fight, they were finally able to board us. They looted and then set fire to the ship. We were taken aboard their vessel and put in the hold, and then, one by one, they began taking us back up on deck. They would search each prisoner, take all of his jewelry and money, and then make him walk the plank.

"I suppose a dozen or so of my shipmates had been pushed into the sea before one of the pirates came down and unfastened my chains, but instead of taking me on deck, he took me to the captain's cabin. There the captain told me that he liked my looks, and if I would join their crew and sign the ship's articles, he would not send me to the bottom of the ocean with the rest of the prisoners. I told him that I wouldn't do it, and I was taken back to the hold.

"When we got back to the hold, the guard fastened my chains again and whispered that if I would accept the captain's offer, he would help me escape from the ship the first time we neared land. I thought it over for a while. The guard seemed like a nice enough sort of fellow, and I thought I could trust him, so I finally had him tell the captain that I would join the crew.

"Things went along all right for the next few days.

70

The captain treated me well. Then one night the guard informed me that there would be an island two miles off the starboard side at midnight. He would divert the attention of the man on watch, so that I could jump over the side and swim to shore. I thanked him and told him that I would be ready when the time came.

"As midnight approached, though, I began to wonder if I could really trust any pirate. I decided that I wouldn't do everything exactly as my friend had told me to do it. I got a large bundle of rags and tied them so that they looked like a man's body, and when I heard the ship's bell strike midnight, I went up on deck and tossed the bundle over the starboard side. Just as I thought might happen, my 'friend' sounded the alarm and there was an explosion of musket fire, aimed directly at the bundle of rags as it drifted by the aft section of the ship.

"While this excitement was taking place on the starboard side, I slid quietly down a rope on the port side, waited a few moments for the ship to move away, and then started swimming for the shore. I made it in about two hours, and at daylight the next morning, I made my way into the town on the island and told them my story.

"As it happened, there was a British merchant ship in the harbor, bound for England, so they took me aboard. When we got to Plymouth, I talked to a representative from the Admiralty and told him what the ship looked like, and the direction in which she was going when I escaped from her. They sent a man-of-war out to try to catch her, but they had no luck. And," he added, smiling at the two midshipmen, "that's all there is to my story."

"Why did he want to get you killed, Mr. Benger?"

71

"I don't know, Henry. He seemed to be quite nice. And I can't tell you what it was that made me distrust him at the last moment before I escaped. He was such an odd fellow—short and dark, and very intelligent, too. His greatest accomplishment—of which he was justifiably very proud—was that he could speak seven or eight different languages, including . . ." Benger jumped to his feet.

"What's the matter?" the boys asked.

"Thomas Rose!" exclaimed Benger. "I *knew* I had seen him somewhere before!"

7

Benger raced to the captain's tent. "Captain! Captain Wilson!" he called, as he threw open the tent's flap.

"What is it?" cried the captain, rising hurriedly. "Are they coming?"

"No, sir," said Benger. "But we are in even more danger than we thought. Mr. Rose is a pirate!"

"A pirate!"

"Yes, sir," said the mate. "I was just telling Henry and Robert White about my capture by pirates and I suddenly realized where I had seen Rose. He was one of the men on that pirate ship."

"There is no doubt about it? It couldn't be a case of mistaken identity?"

"No, sir. Oh, he's changed in these fifteen years, but he's the man, all right."

"But why did he sail with us aboard the *Antelope*? With the exception of a half-dozen or so of the crew, I've sailed with these men for three or four years, and I know that none of them are pirates or are inclined to mutiny. Even if all of the new men *were* pirates, you don't suppose Mr. Rose expected to take the ship with so few men, do you?"

"No, Captain," said Benger. "I think that this is what has probably happened. The *Gazelle* must have been captured by pirates and taken to an island hideaway. Knowing that the East India Company would send out another ship to look for the *Gazelle*, the captain of the pirates' ship probably sent Rose to Macao, with instructions to get himself a place aboard the search ship just to be sure that it did not fail to go to the island where the trap was laid."

"Of course," said Captain Wilson. "Rose could have suggested that we search the island where the pirates are. We would have done it, no doubt, and we would have sighted the *Gazelle*—or the pirate ship, if they have sunk the *Gazelle*. Then they would have snared us with the greatest of ease."

"And they would have two prizes for the price of one," said Benger. "But now what shall we do about Rose? Clap him in irons?"

"No need for that," said the captain. "Like the rest of us, he is not likely to escape from here for some time."

"But, sir," said the mate. "If he knows the language of these natives, he could easily have all of us murdered. Then he could get the natives to take him from one island to the next until he reached his friends, and they could all come back here and collect our arms and ammunition and other valuables."

Seeing that the captain was still not convinced, he added, "Actually, we do not know for sure that he didn't catch up with that scout this afternoon. He might have told him all sorts of lies."

"What you say may very well be true, Mr. Benger," said the captain. "But you must remember that Rose is the only one of us who can talk to these natives. And, frankly, I see very little hope of our getting away from this island unless we are able to get on friendly terms with them. Our ammunition supply is not unlimited, and though we should be able to hold out against them for two or three months, I doubt very seriously that a ship will reach us that soon—if ever."

He paused thoughtfully for a moment. "No," he continued, "we will not put Rose under arrest. We will not even let him know that we suspect him. Now you'd better call Henry and Robert White in here."

The two boys entered the tent. "Gentlemen," the captain said, "Mr. Benger has recognized Mr. Rose as a pirate he once had the misfortune to meet. I must ask that you keep this information entirely to yourselves. We do not want Rose to know that we are aware of his identity. Mr. Benger will tell only the other two mates, and either Mr. Benger, Mr. Barker, Mr. Cummin, or myself will have our eye on Rose at all times. Is that clear?"

"Aye, aye, sir," said the boys. "We won't breathe a word to a soul," Henry added.

"Very well," said the captain. "Will you call Richard Sharp in here, please, Mr. Benger?"

"Aye, aye, sir," said Benger, ducking under the tent's flap.

Richard Sharp was quickly found and brought into the tent. "Mr. Sharp," said the captain. "I am relieving you, at least temporarily, of your duties as cook's helper."

"Yes, sir," said Sharp.

"I have decided to have you three stand your watches on special posts, from which you may be able to warn us of an attack a few moments earlier than if we keep everyone inside the enclosure," said the captain.

"I want each of you to find a tall tree outside the enclosure, but not so far away that you can't return quickly inside the wall if necessary. The moment you see any movement in the forest, shout an alarm, and then get down and back inside the wall as quickly as possible.

"Mr. Sharp, you choose a tree on the side of the enclosure toward the hill. Mr. White, you choose one at the edge of the forest on the west side, and Mr. Wilson, you find one at the edge of the forest on the east side. You can do that at the very first light in the morning."

"That's the most dangerous side," muttered Richard Sharp.

"What's that?" asked the captain, surprised at Sharp's insolence.

"The inland side is the side where the attack is most likely to come," said Sharp. "I don't see why *I* have to be put in the most dangerous position."

"*Mr.* Sharp," said the captain, almost shouting.

"Captain," interrupted Henry, "I should be glad to take that side."

The captain glanced at Henry, and then looked at Sharp, scowling. "Very well, then," he said. "Mr. Wilson, you take the inland side, and you take the east side, Mr. Sharp. That is, *if* you have enough courage to climb a tree!"

The next morning, as soon as it was light enough for them to do so, the three midshipmen set out to find the trees in which each would locate his dry-land "crow's nest."

Henry found a nice, tall coconut palm tree, about one fourth of the way from the enclosure to the spring. He climbed the lower half of it monkey-style, and then, gripping first with his hands and then with his knees, he pulled himself to the top. There, he sat down astride a bunch of green coconuts, each of his feet resting at the base of one of the fronds.

This vantage point gave Henry an excellent view of the surrounding terrain, and it was easy for him to see why his father had decided to send them to stand watches in trees. By leaning around to his left, Henry could barely distinguish Robert White sitting in another coconut palm two or three hundred yards away. Leaning to his right, he could also see Richard Sharp sitting in a smaller tree.

As soon as he was settled, Henry began to move his head slowly from one side to the other, peering into the forest as far as he could see. With his eyes squinting, he would sweep the half-circle of terrain before him from left to right, and then back again from right to left.

The sun rose in the sky, until finally it was beaming in full strength straight down on Henry's head. He began to feel that his head was rapidly swelling to the bursting point. The more his head ached, the tighter Henry's grip became on the fronds. Just as he was beginning to think that he could hold on no longer, he heard Mr. Benger's voice floating up to him from the ground.

"Are you all right, Henry?"

"Yes. Yes, I'm all right," said Henry, taking a new grip on the palm leaf stems.

"You can come down now," said Benger. "We are sending someone to relieve you for a while."

"All right." Henry began to stretch his stiff joints in preparation for the long climb back to the ground.

When he reached the ground, no one was in sight. Benger had gone on to the other midshipmen. Slowly, his whole body aching, Henry started toward the camp, where he could get a badly needed drink of water. Then he remembered that the water in the encampment had not been freshened since the first natives had been sighted, and had begun to taste very stale.

He turned in the direction of the spring, remembering how fresh and cool was its water. Too numb to consider the danger in which he was placing himself, Henry walked into the forest.

The spring flowed from a crack in the face of a low rock cliff on the seaward side of the hill and near its top. Just below the spring was a pool of water about twenty-five feet across at the widest point, and stretching about forty feet from the face of the cliff to where the pond turned into a stream. On either side of the pond there was a clearing about ten or twelve feet wide, carpeted with soft green grass. This ended in a tangle of vines, low bushes, and trees.

In ten minutes Henry reached the pond. He lay on his stomach at its edge and drank his fill of the cool, clear, refreshing water. When he had finished, he sat back in the shade of the trees which overhung the pond and rested happily. He watched some birds fly over from behind him, squawking loudly, and he laughed at their ridiculous sounds.

He lay back and looked at the sky, the bluest sky he had ever seen, and watched a large fleecy white cloud drift idly by. After a few moments, he decided that he had better return to camp. As he got up, Henry tumbled toward the water's edge, catching himself just before he would have fallen in. He lay there for a moment laughing at himself and thinking how cool and wet he would have been if he had fallen into the water.

Now *there* was an idea, he thought. He could strip his clothes off, take a quick, refreshing swim for just a few minutes, and get back to camp before he was missed! Henry jumped to his feet, more carefully this time, and unbuttoned his shirt. He was pulling it off his shoulders when he heard a noise behind him.

Henry spun around.

Standing at the edge of a bush was a boy. He was naked except for a few tattooed designs scattered over his slim brown body.

8

Henry's first thought was to run. He looked quickly in all directions, but so far as he could tell, he and this young native were the only persons anywhere near the spring. He glanced at the other boy and realized that he was just as afraid as he was. This made Henry relax a little and observe the native more calmly.

The boy was quite handsome. His long black hair was rolled into a knot at the crown of his head, and his skin was a golden tan. He was about Henry's height and weight.

Henry began to think that here was his chance to

prove to himself that the friendly approach was best. He took a deep breath, forced himself to smile, and started walking toward the boy.

"*Mora katao!*" said the boy, taking a quick step backwards.

Henry stopped short. Then he took another step forward, and again the boy backed away, saying the same words: "*Mora katao!*"

The boy's voice was so filled with fear and pleading that Henry decided that the words must mean "stay away" or something of that nature. He was at a loss as to what he could do to convince him that he meant him no harm. For a few moments he stood thinking, and then he leaned in the direction of the boy. "Friends," he said, pointing first to the boy and then to himself.

The native did not move an eyelash. He simply stood there, looking as if he might turn at any moment and dash away into the forest.

Taking two or three slow steps backward, Henry sat down on the grass. Then he leaned as far forward as he could and patted the grass with his hand, hoping that the boy would understand that he wanted him to come and sit down with him. He also started talking casually, just as if the young man could understand him.

"I am Henry Wilson," he said. "My father is the captain of the ship which was wrecked on the reef around your island. We want to be friends with you and your people." Henry glanced at the boy and saw that he was beginning to relax.

Taking care not to look too long or hard at him, Henry continued: "We sailed from England. That is an island on the other side of the world. We went to China first, and then we came to these islands to look for another ship which has disappeared."

Henry paused and looked up. He was surprised, and a little frightened, to find that the boy was standing only four or five feet away from him. Swallowing the lump which had risen in his throat, Henry smiled.

A faint smile flickered on the boy's face, and Henry again leaned forward slowly and patted the ground. The native looked at the spot Henry had patted, then he looked back at Henry. Realizing that the boy was not sure what he meant by patting the grass, Henry pointed his finger at him, then pointed to the grass, and then he indicated his own sitting posture.

The native seemed to understand this, and at last he lowered himself slowly into a sitting position on the grass facing Henry. As soon as he was settled, he looked straight at Henry and smiled. This pleased Henry a great deal, and he smiled back at the boy. They sat there for a few moments grinning at each other.

Finally, Henry pointed to himself. "Henry," he said. "Henry."

"Henery?" said the native.

"Hen-ry," Henry said, again pointing to himself.

The boy understood then. He pointed to Henry. "Henery," he said.

"Yes," said Henry. "Hen-ry." Then he pointed to the native.

"Lee Boo," said the boy, pointing to himself. "Lee Boo." Then, again pointing to Henry, he said, "Henery."

"Henry. Lee Boo," said Henry, pointing first to himself and then to the boy.

For a moment the two boys sat silently, then Henry swung his arm in a circle over his head, trying to indicate the island. "Lee Boo, Henry . . . ?" he said, pointing to Lee Boo, himself, and to the ground.

Lee Boo understood perfectly. He pointed to the ground and said, "Oroolong."

"Oroolong?" said Henry.

Lee Boo nodded. "Oroolong," he said again, pointing to the grass. Then, pointing to his left, he said, "Pelew."

Henry did not have any idea where or what "Pelew" was, but it did not interest him too much at the moment, because he had just noticed that Lee Boo's eyes had been fixed almost constantly upon his clothing.

Henry looked down at his shirt and saw that it was closed, but unbuttoned. Deciding to let the breeze blow into his shirt before buttoning it, Henry took the edges of the material in his hands and pulled his shirt front open.

Lee Boo gasped, covering his face with his hands in horror. Henry did not understand why a naked boy should be so horrified at seeing another boy bare his chest, but he closed the front of his shirt and looked at Lee Boo.

Lee Boo slowly uncovered his face. He reached forward cautiously and placed his hand on Henry's chest. His look of horror was replaced by one of puzzlement as he grasped the cloth between his fingers and felt it.

Finally, Henry realized what it was that had so upset Lee Boo. Since he, and probably all of his people, wore

84

no clothing at all, he thought that Henry, too, was naked, and that the clothing was Henry's skin. Naturally, he was horrified to see someone start to remove his own skin!

Henry couldn't keep from bursting into laughter. In a moment, however, Henry stopped. He reached forward and touched Lee Boo's skin, and then he took a piece of his shirt between his fingers, shaking his head from side to side. But Lee Boo did not understand, so Henry pointed to the skin on his own hand, motioning Lee Boo to look closely at it.

Lee Boo leaned forward and his eyes followed Henry's finger as it moved up his hand to his wrist, and then under the cuff of his shirt. The native boy understood then that this top layer was not Henry's skin, but only some sort of covering for the skin. He nodded his head, and then he, too, burst out laughing. He was obviously relieved to learn that this boy was not able to skin himself alive.

Lee Boo took Henry's hand in his own and pointed to the blue veins which showed through the white skin. Then he pointed to his own tattoos. Henry understood that Lee Boo thought that the veins were Henry's tattoos, but he could think of no way to explain to the native what they were, so he simply shook his head. Lee Boo looked puzzled and examined Henry's hand very closely, but he could not imagine what the colored lines were if they were not tattoos, so he shook his head in bewilderment.

The two boys sat facing each other silently for a few moments, then Lee Boo pointed again to his left and

85

said, "Pelew." As he said this, he got to his feet, motion-ing to Henry to follow him.

Henry rose, but he pointed in the other direction toward the camp and motioned to Lee Boo that they should go that way. Lee Boo paid no attention whatever to Henry's motions. He kept pointing to the north and indicating that Henry should follow him.

The two boys stood arguing in sign language for quite a few moments, but then Lee Boo began to look very sad and stopped trying to get Henry to go with him. Henry felt very sorry that he had hurt his new-found friend's feelings. Though his better judgment told him he should return to camp immediately, he finally gave in and indicated to Lee Boo that he would go with him. At this, Lee Boo slapped his thighs gleefully, motioned to Henry to follow, and trotted off into the forest.

At the encampment, Captain Wilson had just finished eating his lunch. "Have the midshipmen come to the tent, please, Mr. Benger," he called.

In a few moments, Richard Sharp and Robert White entered the tent. "Midshipmen Sharp and White report-ing, sir," said Robert.

"Where is Mr. Wilson?" asked the captain, surprised that Henry would be late in reporting for any duty.

"Why, I don't know, sir," said Robert. "I haven't seen him. Have you, Richard?"

"No, I haven't," said Sharp.

"Have you seen him, Mr. Benger?" the captain asked. "You did call him down from his tree, didn't you?"

"Yes, sir," said Benger, "and then I went to these

two lads to tell them the same thing. Didn't he come back to the enclosure?"

"I don't know," said Captain Wilson. "I haven't seen him since he went out to find his tree this morning."

"Well," said Benger. "He's probably around somewhere. I'll find him."

As soon as Benger had gone, the captain turned back to the two midshipmen. "Mr. Sharp," he said, "I noticed that the tree you chose this morning was not very far from the clearing. Do you think that a warning coming from you from that distance would have given us much time to prepare for an attack?"

"It seemed far enough to me, sir," said Sharp.

"I'm sure it did," the captain said. "But the man who was sent to replace you was told to find a higher tree farther from the wall. When you relieve him, I will expect you to use the tree which *he* has chosen."

"But if an attack comes, I might not be able to get back to the enclosure in time," whined Sharp.

"In that case, you can stay in the tree and keep still until the attack is over," said the captain angrily. "You would be as safe there as anywhere."

Benger returned to the tent just then. "He's not inside the wall, Captain," he said. "And none of the men have seen him. The man who took his place in the tree said that Henry was not in sight when he went on duty."

"Where could he be?" asked the captain. "You don't suppose that he could have been captured by the natives between the time that he climbed down from the tree and the time that his replacement reached the tree, do you?"

"I hope not, sir," said Benger. "I have asked Mr. Barker and Mr. Rose to go to the tree and search for signs of Henry."

"Good," said the captain. "Let us meet them and see if they have found anything."

As the two men left the tent, Robert White spoke to the captain. "May I go along with you, sir?" he asked.

"Of course you may," said the captain.

When they had reached the tree where Henry had stood his watch, they met Barker and Rose.

"Any sign of him?" asked the captain.

"Yes, sir," said the second mate. "We found some tracks leading off toward the spring and started to follow them, but we decided to wait for more men, in case we encounter any trouble."

"That's sensible, Mr. Barker," the captain said. "I think that we three will be all you will need, so let us see where the tracks lead."

Following Henry's footprints, the five men strode off toward the spring. At the pond, they spread out to see if they could find anything. It was only a matter of moments before Barker called to the captain. "Sir," he said, "here are some more tracks."

"But these are the prints of a bare foot!" said Robert White.

At that point, Benger said, "I am afraid, sir, that there are some signs of a struggle on the grass near the pond."

"Is there any blood on the grass?" asked the captain.

"No, sir," said Benger.

"They may intend to use him as a hostage, sir," Barker

said. "If they do, then there is a good chance that they won't harm him. Dead hostages are of no use."

"Shall we go back to the camp for some of the men, Captain?" Benger asked. "Perhaps we can find Henry and his captors before dark."

"We will go back to the camp, Mr. Benger," said the captain, "but we will risk no lives, nor the safety of our camp, in such an effort."

"But, sir!" said Benger. "There's hardly a man among the crew who wouldn't risk his own life to save Henry."

"I know," said the captain, "and I am grateful. But if the natives are not going to use him as a hostage, they would kill him before we could even find him; if they do intend to use him as a hostage, they will make an appearance before long, and we can do whatever is necessary to save him then. Now let us get back to camp."

As soon as they reached camp, Captain Wilson went into his tent. All afternoon he worried about Henry. How would he ever be able to face Mrs. Wilson if anything happened to the boy? But then he realized that probably either he and his son would both see home again, or neither one of them would.

Meanwhile, Benger was making the round of the wall, telling the men what had happened. "Unless you are actually attacked," he told them, "hold your fire until the captain or I give the order."

Darkness fell; Benger took Captain Wilson some food. "Thank you, Mr. Benger, but I'm not hungry," said the captain. "I think I shall just try to get some sleep. Goodnight."

"Goodnight, sir."

89

But it was near dawn before the captain finally dropped off to sleep, a sleep filled with dreams of cannibals. It was in the middle of one of these nightmares that the captain was suddenly awakened by Benger's voice shouting, "Hold your fire! Hold your fire!"

The captain rushed outside. "What is it, Mr. Benger?" he asked. The mate pointed. The captain looked down the beach to his right. There, in the first light of dawn, stood fifty or more natives, and in the middle of the front row was Henry.

9

"What shall we do, Captain?"

"Let them make the first move," the captain said. "But you had best get Rose over here so that he can interpret for us."

"Aye, aye, sir."

"Quickly, Mr. Benger!" the captain urged. "They're sending someone toward us now."

Benger looked. "Why, it's Henry and just one guard, sir!"

"It may be a trick. Get Mr. Rose as fast as you can,"

said the captain. "And then keep your eye on those other natives."

In a moment, the mate returned with the interpreter.

"What do you make of this, Mr. Rose?" asked the captain.

Rose surveyed the situation. "I suggest, Captain, that as soon as your son is within reach, we shoot his guard, rush out and grab Henry, and then open fire immediately on them."

Captain Wilson thought this over.

"No, Mr. Rose," said the captain, finally. "We will not open fire on them without provocation. We will wait and see."

"Very well, sir," said Rose. "You are the captain."

A few moments later, Henry reached the wall.

"Henry, my boy!" The captain grabbed him by the shoulders. "Are you all right?"

"Yes, sir," said Henry cheerily. "I know you must have been worried about me, Father, and I am sorry—but I want you to meet Lee Boo before I explain."

"Who?"

"Lee Boo, sir," said Henry, catching Lee Boo by the arm and pulling him over. "His father is the king of this island."

"I'm very happy to meet you, Mr. Boo," said the captain, nodding in Lee Boo's direction. But then, feeling rather silly as he realized that the young man could not understand him, he turned back to Henry. "Where have you been?" he asked angrily.

"Well, sir," said Henry, "I went to the spring yesterday when I came down from the tree—that's where I met Lee

92

Boo. Then I went to the native village with him—it's called Pelew—because I thought we should show the natives that we want to be friendly."

"Were you treated all right?" asked the captain.

"Oh, yes, sir!" exclaimed Henry. "Everyone was very friendly. Aba Tuli—he's Lee Boo's father—let me sleep in his own house, and they fed me some perfectly delicious food."

"Do you have any idea what this Aba Tuli wants?" asked the captain.

"Wants?" said Henry, surprised. "Why, no, sir. Do you think he wants something?"

"We shall see," said the captain, turning to Mr. Rose. "Mr. Rose," he said, "ask Lee Boo here what his father wants."

Rose asked the question and Lee Boo looked surprised that one of these men was able to speak his language. Then a puzzled look came over his face. He said something to Rose, and then he looked at Henry and Captain Wilson, smiling.

"What did he say, Mr. Rose?" asked the captain.

Rose looked at Henry for a moment, and then faced the captain. "He says," said Rose, "that his father, king of the Pelew Islands, wants to be friends with the king of the strange people who have landed on the island of Ooroolong. He says that his father was afraid that the king of the strangers might be worried at his son's absence, so he made everyone arise long before dawn, so that they could get Henry back to you by daylight."

"Tell him," said the captain, "that we, too, wish to be

friends, and that I should like to speak to his father, the king."

Rose translated what the captain had said, and Lee Boo smiled broadly, nodding his head. He motioned for the captain to follow him out to the group of natives who were still standing down the beach.

Captain Wilson nodded his head. "Come along, Mr. Rose," he said. "I will need you to act as interpreter."

"Captain!" exclaimed Rose. "You're not going to go down there, are you? This may well be a trick."

Captain Wilson stopped short. "You may be right," he said. "Perhaps you had better tell Lee Boo to invite his father into the enclosure."

"Yes, sir," said Rose, and he relayed this message to Lee Boo.

Lee Boo nodded and started to walk out of the enclosure. Henry turned, also, to follow Lee Boo, but the captain stopped him. "Where are you going?"

"I'm going with Lee Boo, sir."

"No," said the captain. "You stay here."

"But Father," said Henry. "Aba Tuli may feel the same way you do about going by himself amongst strangers. But if I go back with Lee Boo, then he will know that you trust him."

"Yes," said the captain. "Aba Tuli will know then, that *my* invitation is no trick." He paused thoughtfully for a moment. "That was a wise observation, Henry," he said. "You may go with your friend."

A few minutes later, Henry and Lee Boo returned with Aba Tuli and another native, whom Henry introduced to the captain as Ara Kuka, the king's brother. Captain

Wilson extended his hand to the visitors. Neither of the two men understood what the gesture meant, so Mr. Rose explained to them that the captain wanted to shake hands—a sign of friendship.

Upon hearing this explanation, Aba Tuli and Ara Kuka began shaking hands gleefully with everyone within their reach. The captain waited, amused, until there were no more hands to shake, then he invited the men into his tent.

The entire party—Henry, Lee Boo, Aba Tuli, Ara Kuka, Captain Wilson, Mr. Benger, and Mr. Rose—seated themselves in a circle. Using Rose as his interpreter, Captain Wilson began the long explanation of how he and his men happened to be on the island. He told them how they had left England, which was a large island on the other side of the world, and had sailed to China, which was a huge country to the west of the islands. He told how they had been sent to find another ship like their own which had disappeared, and how the storm had blown them far south of their course and onto the reef.

Aba Tuli waited quietly until the captain was through. Then he turned to Rose and began to speak.

"He wants to know," Rose said, "how people can hang onto the underside of the earth. He thinks it's flat."

"Oh, good heavens!" exclaimed the captain.

"I think I can explain it to them, sir," said Benger. The mate dug into the sand a little way with the side of his boot sole, and then scooped out a handful of wet sand, which he proceeded to shape into a ball. He scratched some lines into it and said to Rose, "Explain to him that the earth is shaped like this, and tell him that this spot is where this island is, and that this other spot is where England is."

Rose explained the crude globe which Benger had made. The three natives nodded their heads in wonder. They seemed to be convinced, however, even though this was a new idea. Aba Tuli spoke to Rose again, and Rose answered him.

"What was that, Mr. Rose?" asked the captain.

"He wanted to know if the object which was on the reef was the boat we used to get here," said Rose. "I told him it was, but he says that it was not very good."

"Ask him if he has any boats as large as that one was," said the captain, slightly irritated.

Rose asked this question of Aba Tuli, and the native king said something and laughed.

"He says that they don't have any that big," said Rose. "But he says that they do have some big boats, not as clumsy as the *Antelope*."

"Ask him how big they are," said the captain.

"He says that he will bring one for you to see tomorrow," said Rose, after getting Aba Tuli's answer. "They had a much bigger one, but it was burned in a raid by natives from a neighboring island."

The men stayed in the tent until midmorning, the captain asking Aba Tuli questions about the island. Aba Tuli told him that the islands were called the Pelews, and that the one which they were on was called Oroolong. The food supply was good on all of the islands, he said. There was plenty of breadfruit, coconuts, plantains, and other fruit, and the lagoons were filled with all sorts of fish that were good to eat.

He told the captain that there were dozens of islands in the group, and that most of them were larger than Oroolong. Some of the islands were not very far away, but others were farther apart, and it took many days to get to them. He also explained that he was the king of about one-third of the islands—the southwestern ones of the group—and that his home was in the village of Pelew on this island. The king of the northern part of the islands was his friend, he said, but the king of the eastern part had attacked Oroolong not very long ago, and so they were at war with each other.

When Captain Wilson asked why the eastern king had attacked Oroolong, Aba Tuli said that he did not know, but that his village had been raided, some of the houses and boats burned, and three of his men had been killed. He asked the captain to show him his spears, so that he could see if they were any better than his own.

The captain motioned to the natives to follow him out of the tent. When they were all outside, he took a musket from one of the men, held it so that the natives could see it, and told Rose to explain that this was their main weapon. Rose translated this to the natives and they crowded around the captain, looking at the gun in disbelief. Finally, Aba Tuli put his finger on the end of the barrel and indicated that it was not even sharp.

Captain Wilson smiled and motioned to them to stand aside. He took careful aim at a sea gull he had seen cruising in the air. When he pulled the trigger, the explosion almost frightened the natives out of their wits, but their fright disappeared as they saw the gull tumble out of the air and fall dead almost at their feet. One of them

97

examined the dead bird and ran excitedly back to his friends, showing them the hole made by the bullet.

Captain Wilson explained how the gun worked, and they were very impressed with the weapon. But they were even more impressed when he took them to one of the cannon and told them that it was the same sort of weapon, only a great deal larger. This was the one, he explained, that they had fired at the canoes.

Aba Tuli said he was grateful to the captain for not making the ball hit any of them. Then he remembered the tools and other objects which they had taken off the ship and said they would return everything.

The captain thanked him. They all shook hands again, and the natives rejoined the group that had been waiting patiently down the beach.

Afterward, the captain addressed his crew. "Men," he said, "though I am sure we need no longer fear an attack, we must watch our behavior and not do anything that might provoke one. One thing which we must do is to guard carefully our materials and supplies. We have many things which these people do not have, and which some of them may try to steal. If they should, or if you find anything missing, come straight to me, and I will take the matter up with the king.

"Above all, do not fight with any of these natives unless one of them attacks you first. We will keep our weapons locked in their cases in the tent from now on, but if you leave the enclosure, you had better get a musket from me to carry with you. Do you have any questions?"

"Aye, sir," said one of the men. "Are we likely to get

home now, Captain, or will we have to spend the rest of our lives on this island?"

"Our chances for getting home are much improved now," said the captain. "The king has told me that they have large canoes—I suppose they must be fifteen or twenty feet long—which can sail from one island to the next. We must hope that there are enough islands close enough together that we will be able to make our way north into a latitude where we are likely to be discovered. I am afraid that we will not be able to sail out of this group of islands in their canoes, though, because it is undoubtedly quite some distance from the northernmost island in this group to the southernmost island in the next. I intend to question the king more closely in this matter when he returns tomorrow."

"But, Captain," said the man, "even the most northern island in this group would probably be far south of the course we were following."

"Yes, that's true," said the captain. "But the farther north we go, the more likely we are to be discovered, and I don't doubt that the ship which looks for us will search for some distance on either side of the course which we were taking. Now let us adjourn for lunch."

Benger followed the captain into his tent. "Captain, that man was right. Even if we get to the northernmost island in this group, we will still be so far south of our original course that there is very little chance of our being found."

"I know," said the captain. "But we must keep up the spirits of the men. It would indeed be foolish for us to give up, now that we have solved the very serious problem of the natives. And we must do everything we can to make it possible for any search ship to find us."

"According to my reading of our position, sir, Yap should be only 150 miles north of us."

"And how many more miles east or west of us?" asked the captain.

"Between fifty and seventy-five miles east, sir," said Benger. "And if this group of islands extends fifty miles to the north, then we would be only a little more than a hundred miles from Yap if we could get to the northernmost of these islands."

"If these islands extended a *hundred* miles north, we would still not be able to sail that other fifty or seventy-five miles to Yap, Mr. Benger," said the captain. "I seriously doubt that the natives' canoe can be sailed out of sight of land."

"Yes, sir, I suppose you are right," said Benger sorrowfully, and he walked slowly out of the tent.

100

10

Early the next morning, Captain Wilson went in search of the cook.

"Mr. Swift," he said, when he had found him, "we must feed the king and his friends today in a manner befitting royalty—even if it is heathen royalty. Now, what do you have in your supplies that might be tasty to a savage tongue?"

"Well, sir," said Swift, who was still of the opinion that all savages were cannibals, "I saved one side of beef from the ship and have been using it very sparingly to make stew. There's still enough left to feed these heathens and us one good meal—that is, if we throw in a goodly portion of yams to fill 'em up with."

"Excellent!" exclaimed the captain. "I'll leave it to you, then, to fix us a first-class banquet."

"Aye, aye, sir," said Swift, and he began bustling around as if he were the chef of the grandest hotel in London.

It was about ten o'clock in the morning when the canoes were first sighted. There were around fifty of them, gliding along in lines, as if they were in a procession. In the middle of them was a large object which looked like a raft with a canopy over it.

A few minutes later, the first canoes slipped by, staying away from the beach so as to leave room for the raft-like object to land. Captain Wilson, standing at the water's edge, called the first mate to him.

"Well, Mr. Benger," he said. "What do you think of *that*?"

Benger squinted in the bright sunlight. "Why, it's two canoes lashed together!" he exclaimed.

"Yes," said the captain. "Two canoes—they must each be forty feet long—fifteen feet apart, with a platform built between them, and a shelter built on top of that."

"And look how she rides in the water, sir," said the mate.

The waves seemed to have almost no effect on the large double canoe. Since one canoe served to balance the other, its pitch and roll was hardly noticeable.

While the mate and the captain had been talking, the

102

double canoe, with Aba Tuli, Ara Kuka, and a few other natives seated under the canopy on the platform, nosed softly into the beach. Aba Tuli jumped down into the knee-deep water between the prows of the two canoes and approached Captain Wilson with his hand extended.

"*Amuno*," said the captain, remembering this word of invitation which Rose had used the first time they had seen one of the natives. "*Amuno*, Aba Tuli."

Aba Tuli smiled broadly at the captain and shook his head vigorously. "*Weel! Weel a trecoy!*" he said.

Captain Wilson looked around for Rose and found him standing beside him. "What did he say, Mr. Rose?"

"He says that he is very pleased, sir."

Aba Tuli spoke again to Rose, and then motioned to the other canoes, which were just coming up onto the beach.

"He says," said Rose to the captain, "that he has told his people that your spears do not need to be thrown in order to kill, but they do not believe him. He wants you to demonstrate the musket again, so that they can all witness it."

"Tell him I shall be very happy to, Mr. Rose," said the captain.

After Aba Tuli and Ara Kuka had shaken hands with everyone near them, the king returned the goods stolen from the ship and apologized again. The captain told Aba Tuli that the incident was now forgotten. Then he led them to his tent and went inside, returning in a moment with two muskets. Aba Tuli motioned for the natives to gather around him, as the captain again explained how the weapon worked. Using Rose to interpret for him,

103

he explained the powder, packing, and ball, as he demonstrated how to load the rifle.

When both rifles were loaded, Captain Wilson said, "Mr. Rose, please tell Aba Tuli to send one of his men down the beach to set up two of those large sea shells in the sand as targets."

While the targets were being placed, the captain handed one rifle to Mr. Benger. "I challenge you to a contest of marksmanship, Mr. Benger," he said, smiling.

"Aye, aye, sir," said Benger, looking down the beach. "But it will not strain the ability of either of us."

"I see what you mean," said the captain, also looking where the native was placing the shells in the sand. "He is putting our targets up not over fifty yards from here."

"Yes," said Benger. "I imagine that is about the effective range of their spears, so it is natural that he would set the targets there."

"Probably," said the captain. "But don't you think it would be a good idea to impress them as much as possible with the effectiveness of our weapons? Let's send him fifty yards further."

"Agreed," said Benger.

The captain motioned to the man to go further away with the shells, and after casting a doubtful glance at the two marksmen, the native picked the shells up and trotted down the beach, looking over his shoulder as he went. The captain kept motioning to him until he was far enough away, then he signaled to him to stop.

The native propped the shells up in the sand, looked at them, looked back toward Benger and the captain, and then stood there with his hands on his hips.

104

"He thinks that he's safe at that distance," said Benger. "He doesn't believe that our 'spears' will ever reach that far."

The captain waved to the native to stand aside. The native, though, simply stood there, grinning broadly. Captain Wilson motioned again for him to stand out of the way.

"May I have your permission to try something, sir?" Benger asked the exasperated captain.

"Why, yes, Mr. Benger," the captain said.

Benger turned to Rose. "Mr. Rose, tell Aba Tuli to call to that native to throw one of those shells into the air."

Rose, a little surprised at this strange request, translated Benger's words for the king, who, in turn, shouted the message to the man down the beach.

The native standing by the shells promptly stooped over and picked one up. He held it in his hand for a moment, looking at it, and finally tossed it into the air about ten feet over his head.

Benger snapped the musket to his shoulder, took aim, and pulled the trigger.

The explosion startled all of the natives, even though they had been warned of the noise the weapon made. Most startled of all, though, was the native who had thrown the shell into the air. He had watched it rise in the air, and then, before his very eyes, it had completely disintegrated, showering him with bits of shell.

For the next few minutes the natives milled around, discussing and re-examining the muskets. While this was going on, Mr. Swift, the cook, walked up. "Captain, may I have a word with you?"

"Certainly," said the captain. "What is it?"

"Sir, I didn't have no idea there would be this many of the natives," he said, "and we don't have enough meat to feed all of them."

"Well, I suppose we will simply have to give them an extra large serving of yams and only a couple of bites of meat apiece."

"Aye, aye, sir," said the cook.

Aba Tuli, though he could not understand English, had been listening with interest. Before Mr. Swift could walk away the native king said something to Rose, and Rose stopped the cook. "Oh, Mr. Swift," he said. "Aba Tuli apparently recognizes you as the cook and has guessed at your problem. He says that only he and his personal party of half a dozen or so will be eating with the captain. The others have brought their own food."

Mr. Swift smiled at Aba Tuli, and then turned to the captain. "I guess they ain't all cannibals after all, sir," he said. "This one here seems to be a right fine, considerate gentleman."

"A true king, I should say, Mr. Swift."

"Captain, the king asked me if I thought you'd like to see his big double canoe more closely," said Rose.

"Yes," said the captain. "Tell him that we will have just about enough time to look at it before lunch."

Rose translated the captain's words for Aba Tuli. The king smiled happily and motioned for the captain, the mate, and Rose to follow him.

When they reached the canoe, which had been pulled halfway up on the beach, the king climbed up to the platform, and then helped the others aboard. The three

Englishmen were immediately surprised by the sturdiness of the flimsy-looking bamboo platform which joined the two canoes together.

"Look at how strongly she's built, Captain!" exclaimed Benger.

"Amazing!" said the captain. "Who would think that such a sturdy vessel could be built out of bamboo, crude rope, and two log canoes?"

"Sir!" said Benger excitedly. "If we had a boat *this* large and strong, we could make it from here to Yap, couldn't we?"

"No, Mr. Benger, I'm afraid not," the captain said. "You are forgetting that there are thirty-three of us. We would need a boat at least half again as large as this before we could safely sail it for any distance."

Benger frowned for a moment; then his face brightened. "But, sir," he said. "Don't you remember that Aba Tuli said he had had a larger boat than this, but it had been burned? Perhaps some of the natives on one of the other islands would have a larger one that we could get by trading some of our supplies."

"We shall see, Mr. Benger," said the captain, turning to Rose. "Mr. Rose, will you ask the king if there are larger canoes on any of the other islands, please."

Rose asked Aba Tuli the question, and then listened quietly to the native's answer. When Aba Tuli had finished, Rose turned back to the captain.

"There are some boats as large as this one," said Rose, "but they belong to the natives with whom he is at war. There are no canoes larger than this one."

"Is that all he said?" asked Benger.

107

"Yes, that is all," said Rose.

"Are you sure?" asked Benger. "It sounded to me like he said a good deal more than that."

"Oh, well, he *did* tell me again that the boat which was burned was larger than this one," said Rose, looking away from Benger's steady gaze.

Afraid that Benger might give away the fact that they were suspicious of Rose, Captain Wilson interrupted. "Well," he said, "I think we've seen all that we need to see. And lunch is probably ready, so let us go back to the tent."

Benger looked steadily at Rose for a moment more, and then turned without a word, jumped down onto the beach, and walked off toward the enclosure.

"Tell Aba Tuli that we are very impressed with his boat, Mr. Rose," said the captain. "And thank him for showing it to us."

When Aba Tuli, Ara Kuka, Benger, Rose, and the captain went inside the tent for lunch, the king looked very shocked and said something to Rose. The two of them talked to each other rapidly for a few moments.

"And what was *that* all about, Mr. Rose?" asked Benger.

"He said," said Rose, "that he was surprised at seeing the meat on his plate. He thought it was human meat, and was disappointed at finding that we were cannibals. I told him that the meat came from a four-legged animal that was kept for eating purposes, but he has never seen any animals other than humans, fish, and birds, so it is a little hard for me to explain to him."

"Since he recognized this as flesh," said the captain, "he must be a cannibal."

108

"He says that his people stopped eating their dead enemies before he was born," Rose said. "But he has seen human flesh cooking in enemy villages during the course of battles."

"Let's hope," said the captain, "that they don't take up the habit again—at least while we are here."

The three Englishmen laughed, and the natives joined in, even though they had no idea what the cause of the laughter was.

"Does he like the meat now that he knows it isn't human flesh?" the captain asked.

Rose and the king spoke together for a moment. "He says he likes fish better," said Rose, "but that this is better than the meat of birds."

"It's a shame we couldn't have saved some of the animals from the ship," the captain said. "We shall all probably get very tired of fish and birds before we get off this island."

"Could we ask him how large the boat was that burned?" asked Benger.

"Why, yes, of course," said the captain, nodding to Rose.

Aba Tuli listened attentively to Rose's question, and then looked at the captain for a moment before answering. He had been very proud of his large boat, so he wanted to answer the captain directly. He drew a picture of a canoe in the sand with his finger. Pointing to the picture, and then pointing out of the tent toward the canoe in which he had come, he indicated that the picture was supposed to be of his present canoe. Below the picture he had already drawn in the sand, he drew

109

another canoe almost twice as large as the first. He pointed to the second drawing, and then made upward motions with both hands to describe flames.

"Does he mean that the canoe that burned was almost twice as long as that canoe out there?" asked the captain, hoping that he had not misunderstood.

"Yes, sir," said Rose, after consulting with the king for a moment. "That is what he means."

The captain and Benger were speechless. They had supposed that the canoe which had burned had been three or four feet longer than the present canoe, but now it appeared that the old canoe had been at least seventy feet long!

The captain turned to Rose. "Ask him if it would be possible to build such a boat again," he said. "Tell him that we will have to have one that large before we can hope to return to our home."

Rose asked the king this question, and then told the captain, "He says that one could be built. They have already found two trees tall enough and straight enough to make the canoes from. They were planning to use them to make a new canoe for the king, but he says that he will let you have them, and will even have some of his people help us to build it."

"Wonderful!" shouted Benger. "We can get to Yap!"

Rose interrupted Benger to say that Aba Tuli had just said that it would take two or three months to build such a boat, if everyone worked hard.

"Do you think that the search boat—if they send one— will have gone past Yap in that length of time, Captain?" asked Benger, a worried look coming over his face.

"Considering the route we planned to follow when we left China, Mr. Benger, they probably won't even know that we're lost for eight months—or maybe a year!"

"Well," said Benger, embarrassed at having asked such a foolish question, "we'll have a long, hard wait on Yap."

"Yes," said the captain. "We would have a long wait on Yap—if we were going there."

"What do you mean, sir? If we are not going to Yap, then where *are* we going? Farther north into the Carolines group?"

"To Macao," the captain said.

11

Two days later, a month to the day from the time
the *Antelope* had sailed out of the harbor at Macao, the
two tall trees were felled. Then began the tedious
building process which would take many weeks of tiresome labor.

First, the limbs had to be trimmed carefully from the
trunks of the two trees. They had to be dragged to the

water and floated to the Englishmen's camp, and there the bark had to be stripped from the trunks piece by piece. The natives had to show the Englishmen how to do everything, for every step in the building of the two canoes had to be performed with the greatest of care. A single slip could destroy the balance or straightness of the canoe and make it useless, and trees that were tall enough and straight enough to make such canoes were very hard to find. Because of this, shaping the trunks and hollowing them out had to be done by hand with small hatchets and knives, rather than the larger axes which the Englishmen had.

Only about half of the men could work on the canoes at one time, so it was a long, slow process, with each man working only every other day. Later on, when the boat was nearly finished, these "off days" would be spent in getting the supplies ready for the voyage. Until that time, though, the men were allowed to fish, to swim, or explore, or do whatever they wished on the days when they were not working on the two canoes. The only restriction placed upon them was that they were not to go near the native village, or even associate with the natives outside the enclosure.

"Our situation now," the captain told the men, "is excellent. I do not intend to allow any of you to do anything that would jeopardize our position, so I make you this promise: If any of you disregard my orders and get into trouble with the natives, I shall turn you over to Aba Tuli. I will not raise a hand to protect you from any punishment which he considers to be just."

Henry, however, had been invited back to the village

by Lee Boo, and the captain decided that the rule would not apply to the three midshipmen. These young lads, he thought, would make friends with the young natives, and would probably strengthen the Englishmen's position on the island. And if they did do something wrong, Aba Tuli would no doubt think of it as just a youthful error.

A few days later, then, Henry sent word to Lee Boo by one of the natives that he did not have to work the next day and would come to the village to visit him.

The next morning, Henry arose early, had breakfast, and then set out for the northwest shore of the island, where the village of Pelew was located. About an hour later, he stood on the top of a hill, looking down upon the neat, clean village, with the small stream flowing along its northern edge. Another twenty minutes found Henry at the edge of the village, and the sounds of the natives gathering around him immediately brought Lee Boo and his father out of their house to meet him.

Although Henry had already spent one night at Pelew, he had been looked upon then as a curiosity. This time, however, he was welcomed as a friend and treated royally. He was shown all over the village. He had come just before dark on his first visit and had not been able to see very much of it.

Lee Boo was his guide, and he took Henry to his father's house first. It was fairly large, made mostly of bamboo, and with a thatched roof of coconut fronds. It had no floor, but large mats woven of palm leaves covered the sand, making the inside neat and tidy. There were no windows or doors in any of the houses. Instead, the houses were made so that all four sides, or parts of them, could be removed, depending upon how warm the weather was.

Henry marveled at the fact that all of the houses were left open nearly all of the time, even when the owners were gone. But then, he thought, why shouldn't they leave them open? There was no reason for anyone to want to steal anything. Food was growing freely all over the island. The few personal items that the natives owned, such as spears and fish hooks of bone, and other tools, were made during the many free hours that the natives had, and they seemed to look upon these little jobs as pleasant diversions.

As a matter of fact, during the many hours that Henry spent at Pelew, he never once saw any of the natives working. Not that things did not get done. On the contrary, houses were built, mats were woven, small canoes were made, coral walks were laid, and fishing nets were repaired. It was just that none of these things seemed like work when the natives did them.

When a new house was being built, everyone joined in to help, and from the laughter and chattering that went on, you would have thought that the natives were playing a game rather than building a house. But a house would get built, and quickly at that. And everyone saw to it that it was as nice and as large and as well built as any other house in the village.

The thing that amazed Henry most that morning, as he walked through the village with Lee Boo, was the neatness of the place. Any dead leaf or other bit of trash that might appear was immediately picked up and buried in the sand by the first person who saw it. This was very different from the way it was in Plymouth, where everyone dumped his trash and garbage into the streets and let it lie there and rot.

Lee Boo interrupted Henry's thoughts. *"Munga,* Henery," he said, making motions as if he were eating.

Henry followed his young friend back to his house and found a meal of breadfruit, plantains, and fish waiting for them. After tasting of each of the dishes, Henry decided that Ludee, Lee Boo's mother, was as good a cook as she was beautiful. She was of medium height and was slightly plump, with large brown eyes, golden-tan complexion, and long black hair, piled casually on top of her head and held there with a comb made of fish-bone. Henry thought that she must have been only about her son's age when Lee Boo was born, for she certainly did not appear as old as his own mother back in England. And Henry noticed that even the tattoo marks which ran across her shoulders and down each arm did not detract from her beauty.

When they had finished eating, Lee Boo got up, took Henry's arm, and led him to a far corner of the house. There he pointed to a pile of mats which were lying on the ground, saying, *"Adapat,* Henery," and he made signs that Henry should lie down and go to sleep. As Henry was to learn, in that village they ate whenever they happened to get hungry, and they nearly always took a short nap after they had eaten.

Both boys lay down on the mats, and Lee Boo was asleep almost immediately. Henry lay looking out through the open walls of the house at the palm trees swaying in the breeze until the soft, cool wind blowing over him made him drowsy, and he, too, dropped off to sleep.

It was shortly after noon when Henry awoke, with Lee Boo tugging at his sleeve and calling, "Henery, Henery."

Henry sat up. Lee Boo pointed toward the front of the house, smiling broadly. Henry looked in that direction and was surprised to see Richard Sharp standing there. He got to his feet, and he and Lee Boo walked to the front of the house.

"*Weel! Weel a trecoy!*" said Lee Boo happily.

"Hello," said Henry to Sharp. "What are you doing here?"

"Oh, I was just wandering around and saw the village down here," Sharp said. "So I thought I'd just come down and see what it looked like."

Lee Boo held up his hand to indicate that they should wait there, then he said, "*Malil,*" and ran back to the other end of the house, where they had been sleeping.

"What does '*malil*' mean?" Sharp asked Henry.

"I don't know," Henry answered. "But I guess we'll find out in a moment," he added, as Lee Boo returned with a sharkskin pouch and motioned to the two boys to follow him.

Lee Boo stopped a few yards from the house in the shade of a big tree, knelt down, and smoothed out the sand. He drew a circle in the sand, stood up, shook what looked like some round, white pebbles into his hand from the pouch and dropped them into the circle. Then he gave one of them to Henry, and one to Sharp, and said, "*Malil,*" pointing to the circle.

118

"Why, he wants us to play marbles with him," said Henry, surprised that the game was known even on this remote island.

"Marbles!" said Sharp, his eyes bulging as he looked at the small, round, white object which Lee Boo had handed him. "This is a *pearl!*"

"A pearl!" exclaimed Henry, looking at the little white ball in his own hand.

"These marbles are worth a fortune!" Sharp said excitedly.

Henry looked at Lee Boo and saw that he was bewildered by his and Sharp's excitement, so he turned back to Sharp.

"Well," he said, "they are not ours, and it doesn't look like the natives think they're very valuable, so we might as well go on and play with them."

Lee Boo motioned for them to watch him. Henry nodded his head vigorously to try to make Lee Boo understand that he already knew how the game was played, but Lee Boo just smiled, nodded back at Henry, and proceeded to step off fifteen paces from the edge of the circle. When he had measured the correct distance, Lee Boo drew a straight line in the sand and again motioned to Henry and Sharp to watch him.

Henry looked at Sharp and shrugged his shoulders, as if to say that they might as well watch, even though they already knew how to play.

Both boys watched as Lee Boo drew back his arm and hurled his pearl at the circle. Much to the surprise of the two English boys, Lee Boo's pearl hit another pearl in the ring, and both of them bounced out of the

119

circle. Lee Boo ran forward and picked up both pearls; then he indicated that it was Henry's shot.

Henry stepped up to the line, and though he preferred the English method of "shooting" marbles rather than throwing them, he threw his pearl as Lee Boo had done. His hit the circle, but it bounced out without touching any of the other pearls, and Lee Boo motioned for Sharp to try his luck.

As Sharp came up to the line, he turned to Henry and grinned. "Do you suppose he wants to play for 'keeps'?" he asked.

"No!" said Henry. "And you'd better be sure that you give all of them back to him, too."

Sharp did not answer, but took careful aim and let his pearl fly. He was far wide of his mark, though, and his pearl did not even hit near the circle, so Lee Boo took another shot and again knocked another pearl out of the ring.

It did not take long for Lee Boo to realize that the two English boys were not very good at this game—neither of them could even hit in the circle after the first throw— so the young native shook his head sadly and put the pearls back in his pouch. He then motioned to them to follow him and trotted off in the direction of a tall coconut palm. Before either Henry or Sharp could catch up with him, Lee Boo had climbed halfway up the tree. He stopped there, motioning for them not to follow him, and then climbed to the top, where he cut three ripe coconuts loose and watched them plummet to the ground. He climbed back down the tree quickly, cut each of the nuts open, and began drinking from his own.

Neither Henry nor Sharp had tasted coconut milk before. They took a careful first sip. Much to their surprise, the juice tasted wonderfully sweet and cool, and they drank the contents in three or four big gulps.

After this refreshment, the three boys returned to the king's house. Lee Boo went to the back of the house, where his mat lay, to put away his "marbles." He undid a string which came down from the rafters supporting the roof and was tied to one of the posts near his mat, and let it slide through his fingers until a large pouch fastened to the other end descended from the ceiling. Then he put the small pouch with the pearls in it into the larger pouch, and pulled on the string until the pouch had risen to its usual place up against the high roof of the house.

The three boys wandered around the village then, with Lee Boo teaching Henry and Sharp the Pelewan names for the objects which they saw, and Henry would tell Lee Boo the English name for each of them. After some time, Henry said they must return to the Englishmen's cove. Lee Boo indicated to Henry that he would row them back in his canoe. Henry smiled and nodded, and Lee Boo ran in the direction of the small inlet where his canoe was kept and motioned for them to follow.

"Come on," Henry said to Sharp. "He's going to row us back to the camp."

"Oh," said Sharp, "I think I'll—uh—I'll walk back. You see I was—uh—that is, I want to stop by the spring on my way back."

"Well," Henry said, frowning, "you'd better hurry. It will be dark soon."

121

"Oh, I'll be back in plenty of time," Sharp said, as he turned and started walking toward the forest.

The next morning, as Henry was looking for the tools which he would use in hollowing out the log canoe, his father came up to him.

"Where is Mr. Sharp?" he asked.

"Why, I don't know, sir," said Henry. "Isn't he here?"

"Well, he wasn't at breakfast, and I haven't seen him anywhere else," the captain said.

"I'll see if he is in his tent," Henry said, running toward the tent in which Sharp was supposed to sleep.

When he entered the tent, Henry found Sharp sitting in the sand with his back to the entrance and examining something which he hid quickly as soon as he heard Henry enter.

"What was that?" Henry asked.

"What was what?" said Sharp innocently.

"What did you have in your hands when I came in?" Henry demanded suspiciously.

"Why, nothing," Sharp said. "I didn't have anything. I was just looking at the blisters on my hands."

Suddenly, Henry became wild with rage. He grabbed Sharp by the shirt front and dragged him to his feet and out of the tent.

"You come out of there and show me what you were looking at!" Henry shouted.

Sharp doubled up his fist and hit Henry in the chest, knocking him sprawling in the sand. They rolled and tumbled in the sand, first one on top, then the other.

Henry managed to get to his feet, and the two boys

122

faced each other like boxers. Henry finally charged in and jammed his fist into Sharp's stomach, doubling him up. But then Sharp landed a solid blow on Henry's eye and knocked him down again, and again they rolled and tumbled in the sand.

At that point, the captain and some of the men heard the sounds of the fighting and came running toward the two boys. When they got there, Henry was on top of Sharp and had both of his arms pinned to the ground. Lying in the sand nearby was the little bag of pearls.

"I knew that was what it was," Henry shouted as the men pulled them apart. "You stayed behind so that you could steal Lee Boo's pearls! You thief! I should have known that was what you were going to do!"

Henry snatched the pouch of pearls from the sand. "These belong to Lee Boo, and Sharp stole them last night."

The captain opened the little bag and poured its contents out into his hand. "You say these belong to Lee Boo?"

"Yes, sir," said Henry. "They're his marbles."

"Marbles!" said Benger and the captain.

"Yes, sir," Henry said. "Sharp and Lee Boo and I played marbles with them yesterday, and I should have known that he would steal them if he had half a chance."

"Why, they would be worth a fortune back in England," said Benger.

The captain turned to Sharp. "Is it true?" he asked. "Did you steal these?"

Sharp lowered his head until his chin rested on his

123

chest. "Yes, sir," he admitted, speaking so quietly that the captain could hardly hear him.

Captain Wilson turned to the men who were crowding around. "When I gave permission for the midshipmen to visit the village, I had no idea that any of them would be capable of doing such a thing as this. Since one of them has seen fit to violate the spirit of my order, I shall keep my promise. I am going to return these pearls to their rightful owner and turn Mr. Sharp over to Aba Tuli to do with as he sees fit. I just hope that he will be lenient because of the boy's age," he added, looking grimly at Sharp.

Turning back to the men, he said, "We may be able to buy some from them fairly cheaply before we go, but we will not take one pearl from this island unless we can come by it honestly.

"Mr. Benger, you and Mr. Rose come with Henry and Mr. Sharp and me. We are going to take these pearls back. I hope that you have not damaged our position on the island beyond repair," he added, looking at Sharp.

Not a word was spoken by any of the five on the long walk between the camp and the village. When Aba Tuli greeted them in front of his house, the captain wasted no time in explaining why they were there.

"Mr. Rose," he said, "please tell the king that this boy stole these pearls yesterday, and that we are returning them to him. Tell him that they are very valuable in our country, and that we are very angry at the boy for having stolen them. Say that we agree to whatever punishment he thinks the boy deserves."

Rose protested. "Sir," he said, "if we tell him that these

pearls are valuable, the natives will want a higher price for them when we try to buy them."

"I said, Mr. Rose," the captain said sternly, "that we were going to be honest with these natives, and I mean for us to be completely honest. Now tell him what I said —and don't underestimate the value of the pearls when you describe their worth to him."

"Very well, Captain," Rose said. Then he translated the captain's message to Aba Tuli, as the captain handed the pearls back to Lee Boo.

The native looked at the pearls, and then smiled broadly, speaking for a moment to Rose.

"What did he say, Mr. Rose?" asked the captain.

"He says that they are just trinkets, and that there are plenty more of them in the oysters in the lagoon," said Rose.

"Tell him," the captain said, "that this is a very serious matter. Explain to him that if anyone in our country had stolen these pearls and been caught, he would be killed."

As Rose relayed this message to the king, Aba Tuli's smile slowly disappeared, and his face grew very grave. He spoke a few words to Rose, took the pouch from Lee Boo's hands, and extended it toward Sharp.

"He says," said Rose, "that he now understands the seriousness of the matter, and he wants to give the pearls to Sharp. He says that if you have something someone wants badly enough to steal, then you should give it to him, so that you won't make a thief of him."

"Well," said the captain. "I have never heard *that* argument before." Then he turned to Sharp. "You have heard what Mr. Rose said. The king is offering to give

125

you the pearls. You have my permission to take them."

Sharp looked at Aba Tuli for a moment, and then he looked at Lee Boo and Henry. He glanced at Aba Tuli's outstretched hand with the bag of pearls in it. "I can't take them!" He walked away.

The captain stared after Sharp. He looked around at Aba Tuli and saw that a soft smile was on the king's lips.

"Well, gentlemen," said the captain, "it appears that these people know more about human nature than we do. I doubt that any punishment would have been as effective. Will you thank him, please, Mr. Rose."

While Rose thanked Aba Tuli, Henry ran to catch up with Sharp. The boy only looked at Henry and did not say anything.

Henry walked along beside him for a few moments, and then said, "Richard, I don't know why we haven't got along with each other. Both Robert White and I have wanted to be friends with you."

After a moment, Richard asked Henry timidly, "Do you *really* want to be friends with me?"

"Of course we do. We always have."

Richard stopped and faced Henry. "Thank you, Henry," he said. "I'd like that very much."

They shook hands, and then started walking again. "Oh, by the way," Richard said, after a few moments. "Do you remember my telling you that I had been on two voyages before this one?"

"Yes, I remember."

"Well," Richard said, blushing slightly. "They were both to Portugal."

"To Portugal!" Henry exclaimed. "Then you haven't

126

had any more experience as a midshipman than I have, after all."

"No."

Thinking of how jealous he had been of Richard, Henry threw his head back and laughed aloud. After a moment, Richard joined in, and the two boys walked arm in arm into the forest.

12

Shortly after lunch that same day, while Henry was
working on one of the canoes, Benger came around to
see him.

"How is your eye?" asked the mate.

"Well, it is rather sore," Henry answered, putting his
hand gingerly to the eye which Richard had hit during
the fight that morning.

"It's a beautiful shade of black."

Henry smiled. "I was afraid it would be," he said.

"Tell me something, Henry," Benger said. "Why didn't
you use that fighting technique I showed you on the ship?

If you had, you wouldn't be nursing that black eye."

"I forgot all about it, Mr. Benger," said Henry.

"Forgot!" exclaimed Benger. "That's a fine thing!"

"But I never did learn how to do it very well," Henry protested. "Don't you remember? Every time I tried to kick the wall on the ship, all I did was fall down."

"That's why I was hoping you'd try it in your fight this morning," Benger said. "Necessity often helps us to do things which we don't think we can do."

"Well," said Henry, a little uncertainly, "I'll try to remember next time."

"Just remember that you only need room to take a couple of steps before you jump into the air," Benger said. "And falling to the ground after you've kicked is not going to hurt you nearly as much as getting that black eye did." He slapped Henry on the back. "Now get back to work," he said, smiling.

One night a few days later, Henry went to his father's tent. "Father," he said, "may Richard and Robert and I go to Pelew tomorrow to see Lee Boo?"

"Do you think it wise for Richard to go to the village after what has happened?" the captain asked.

"Oh, yes, sir," Henry said. "I think he has learned his lesson. He has been much nicer since the day we returned the pearls."

"Yes," the captain said thoughtfully, "and he has been working harder than almost any other man on his canoe."

"I'm sure that Lee Boo and Aba Tuli have forgiven him for everything," said Henry.

130

"I suppose you're right, my boy. Tell me, did Richard ask you to ask me if he could go?"

"Oh, no, sir," Henry said. "He doesn't even know that I'm planning to go."

"Maybe he won't want to go with you," the captain said.

"I think he will," said Henry. "I think he'll want the chance to show the natives how he has changed."

"All right, then, go ahead."

The next day, and on many occasions after that during the next several weeks, the three midshipmen went to visit in the home of Aba Tuli. Together with Lee Boo, they explored the whole island; they swam and fished at all of the good beaches; they climbed the island's three hills and looked off into the distance where they could see other islands dotting the horizon.

But most of all, they liked to sit on the high cliff on the northeast side of the island and watch the breakers pound into the reef. It was a beautiful sight, the breakers were so white, and the water was such a deep blue that it looked almost like ink.

The first two or three times they visited Lee Boo, he enticed them into various games. They had races, both running and swimming. They threw rocks at targets, and Lee Boo even tried to show them how to throw spears. But in all these games, Lee Boo was by far the best. Finally he stopped challenging them, and started thinking of other things for them to do in which the English boys could hold their own. He still tried to teach them such things as spear throwing and diving, but he

131

would no longer compete with them. After showing them how, he would stand by and watch them compete with each other.

The boys tried to learn the Pelewan language, but as time went on, first Robert and then Richard lost interest. It was a complicated language, and Henry was the only one who made any headway at all. Every time they had the chance, he and Lee Boo would sit down together and teach each other their native tongues. And Lee Boo was learning English just about as rapidly as Henry was learning Pelewan.

Naturally, as each of the two boys became more and more familiar with the other's language, they talked about more and more things. Using both languages, Lee Boo told Henry some of the legends of his people, of how they had come to these islands from other islands far to the north, using only the stars to guide them.

In turn, also using both languages, Henry described the world to Lee Boo, telling him what the different countries were and where they were. Lee Boo's people had always thought that the world was just one huge ocean with islands scattered over it. That there could be land masses as large as the continents which Henry described was all but unbelievable.

In this way, Henry and Lee Boo spent many, many pleasant hours together, and when Henry finally came to Aba Tuli's house and told Lee Boo that the boat was almost finished, and that they planned to sail in another ten days, the native boy was very sad. Since Henry had broken the news to Lee Boo in Pelewan, Aba Tuli, who had been sitting nearby, understood him and came over

132

to the two boys. He put his arm around his son's shoulders, and then turned to Henry.

"I would like your father and his friends to come to a feast which we are having in three days," he said to Henry in Pelewan. "I want to ask him to do two things for me."

"I shall be glad to tell him of your invitation when I go back this afternoon," Henry answered.

"Thank you," said the king. Then he turned to his son. "Lee Boo," he said. "Do not be sad. I have a very big present which I am going to give you when these people leave."

"What is the present, Father?" Lee Boo asked.

"I cannot tell you until it is time for the English to leave," said Aba Tuli. "But it will make you happy again."

"All right, Father," said Lee Boo.

The two boys started toward their favorite spot—a cliff some half mile away across the tip of the island. When they reached the top of the cliff, they sat down on the grass. Neither of them spoke for some time.

Occasionally, Henry would throw a rock out into the air and watch it plummet the hundred or more feet to the water, but mostly they just sat and looked out over the wide, beautiful, peaceful Pacific.

"I do not want you to leave, Henery," said Lee Boo, finally, in his own language. "But I understand why you must go."

"Yes, I must go," Henry said. "I wish you could go with us."

"I would like that very much," Lee Boo said. "I would like to see all those things you have told me about, the

133

cities and buildings and animals. But it is so far away that my father would never let me go."

"No, I guess he wouldn't," Henry said. Then he rose quickly to his feet. "Well, let's throw spears or run a race or go swimming or something," he said, almost angrily. "There is no use sitting here and talking all day."

Three days later, in the late afternoon, the captain, his three mates, Mr. Rose, and Henry arrived to take part in the feast at Pelew.

Aba Tuli conducted them on a tour of the village amid the noisy preparations which were still going on, and ended the tour at the center of the village.

There, for the feast to come, palm leaves had been spread thickly upon the ground with all of the fresh fruits and vegetables which grew on the island arranged in neat piles down the center. Aba Tuli showed them where they would sit—the captain at his right, Henry at his left—and the others spread down either side of the table. Mr. Rose, being the interpreter, was to sit next to Henry.

Then Aba Tuli took the men to his house to show them the treasures which had been handed down from father to son in the long line of kings which had preceded him. Among these things were a small dagger carved from a single piece of shark's jawbone, and a necklace of shark's teeth, to which a tooth had to be added for each year of a king's reign.

"Why, there must be five or six hundred teeth on that string," exclaimed Benger. "Does the king have to kill the shark himself?"

"Yes," said Rose. "I have heard of this custom. It seems that they believe that when a king is so old he can no longer kill a shark by himself, then he is too old to be king. He must hand his throne to a son, who must kill one. If his son can't kill a shark within a certain length of time, then the people choose a man from among themselves. If he kills a shark within the proper time, he becomes king."

"That seems to be a fairly reasonable requirement," said Captain Wilson.

"I doubt that King George would agree with you, sir," said Benger, laughing.

The captain laughed, too. "I meant that it was a reasonable requirement for people living under these conditions, of course."

The next item which Aba Tuli showed them was a model of a twin-hulled boat, such as the one the Englishmen were building. He explained that it was a scale model of the boat which had brought the original inhabitants to these islands from their former home far to the north. They had discovered the island group, and some of them had returned home to guide others back to their new home.

"How did they ever find their way back?" the captain asked.

"They navigated by the stars," Rose answered. "It took thirty-six days for them to make the voyage from that island to this group."

"And why did they want to leave their old home?" asked the first mate.

"The other islands were becoming too crowded," Rose

135

said. "The population was too large for the food supply."

"Our voyage to Macao should take about the same length of time," said the captain. "And if they could do it, so can we."

One of the natives in charge of the preparation of the meal told Aba Tuli that all was ready. The king motioned for the group to follow him.

As soon as they were seated at the feast, the captain asked Aba Tuli about his two requests, but the king refused to discuss them during the feast. Instead, he insisted that they pass their time in eating and in idle chatter. This polite conversation was kept up during the native dances which accompanied the serving of the last course.

When all the food had been eaten, and the musicians were sitting before the fire playing on their flutes and other crude instruments, the king opened the subject of his requests.

"The king says he has two requests to make of you," said Rose, "and he says that you must not feel obliged to fulfill his first request if you think that it will prevent your safe departure from the island."

"And what is this first request?" Captain Wilson asked.

Rose listened carefully to Aba Tuli's answer to this question, and then he looked from the king to the captain, and back again several times, without translating what Aba Tuli had said.

"Well, what is it?" the captain said, irritated at Rose's delay.

"He says that he is going to engage the natives on another island in battle," said Rose. "They are the natives who raided this village some months ago, and he has been preparing to get his revenge ever since. He wants me to arm some of our men with our weapons and help them. With our weapons, he says, there will be no trouble or danger in defeating them."

"He wants *you* to lead a group of our men into battle?" the captain asked, surprised.

"Yes," said Rose, speaking more hurriedly. "He says that he doesn't want to ask you or any of the ship's officers because he doesn't want to delay our work on the boat."

"Tell him that I will lead a group myself," said the captain.

Rose spoke to Aba Tuli for a moment and then turned back to the captain. "He says that if any of the officers were to go, he would feel that he had imposed on you. He would rather fight without your help than to feel that he had done that."

The captain looked at Benger to see if he had any suggestions to offer, but the mate just sat silently and stared at Rose. "Well," said the captain finally. "I suppose that you may tell him that we will cooperate."

Rose translated this for Aba Tuli, and the chief looked at the captain and smiled, shaking hands with him vigorously.

"What is his second request, Mr. Rose?"

Rose asked Aba Tuli this question, and then turned back to the captain. "He says that one thing at a time is enough," said Rose. "He doesn't want to make his second request until the first has been carried out."

"Oh. Very well, then."

In a short while, the musicians disappeared, Aba Tuli said goodnight to his guests, and the Englishmen trudged off into the moonlit forest. With no clouds to hide it, the moon looked like a blue-white sun. It was so bright that the men had no trouble at all in finding their way back to camp.

As soon as they had said goodnight, the captain asked Benger to step into his tent for a moment.

"What do you think of arming Rose and some of the other men to send along with Aba Tuli?" he asked the mate as soon as they were inside.

"I don't like it at all, sir," said Benger.

"But if one of us chose the men to go along with him, we could at least trust *them*," said the captain. "We can't afford to refuse Aba Tuli's request after all he has done for us."

"Father," said Henry, entering the tent suddenly.

"Yes, Henry?" the captain asked. "I thought you had gone to bed."

"No, sir," said Henry. "I have to tell you something."

"Well, what is it?" said the captain. "Can't you see that Mr. Benger and I are busy?"

"Well, sir, Mr. Rose didn't tell you the truth when he translated what Aba Tuli said. You see, Lee Boo has been teaching me their language. I haven't told anybody because I wanted to surprise you. I've learned it fairly well, as Robert and Richard can tell you."

"You mean you've learned their language during those visits to the village?" the captain asked, amazed.

"Yes, sir," said Henry. "And Lee Boo has been learning English, too."

138

"Remarkable!" said the captain. "But what did Aba Tuli really say, then, Henry?"

"He asked if *you* would arm some men and lead them into battle for him."

"What did Rose say to the king?" Benger asked.

"He told him that you said you were too busy, and that you wanted to know if he would mind if Rose led the men. Aba Tuli said he would take any leader you chose, and that he hadn't meant to impose on your time," Henry explained.

"He could have made the king think that we had insulted him by refusing his request!" exclaimed the captain.

"Yes," said Benger. "So far as the king knows, we have refused to lead the group ourselves and have offered him a mere passenger as a leader. What an ill-mannered lot Aba Tuli must think us."

"Henry," said the captain, taking his son by the shoulders, "in the morning, first thing, you go as fast as your legs will carry you to the village and tell Aba Tuli that the captain misunderstood what it was that he wanted. Tell him that the captain will have men armed and ready to go whenever the king wishes, and that the captain will lead the men himself."

"Yes, sir," said Henry.

"And remember, both of you," the captain said, "Rose mustn't find out that you know the native language, Henry, or he will know that he's suspected. It also means that we will have to think of a good reason for my leading the men instead of letting him lead them."

"Yes," said Benger. "We'll have to think of it fast, too."

"Now let's go to bed, and perhaps things will look brighter in the morning," the captain said.

"Aye, aye, sir. Goodnight." Benger and Henry left the tent.

13

The next morning, Henry was awakened by his father. "Henry," the captain said, "I want to talk to you before you go to Pelew this morning."

After he had dressed and had breakfast, Henry went to his father's tent to see what it was the captain wished to talk to him about.

"Oh, come in, my boy," said the captain. "Sit down for a moment."

Henry sat down and made himself comfortable.

"I think," the captain said, "I've hit upon a plan to keep Rose from discovering that you knew he was lying last night. At the same time it will give me the opportunity to take command of the armed group. Did you say that Lee Boo has learned to speak English?"

"Yes, sir."

"And does he speak it very well?" the captain asked.

"He speaks English almost as well as I speak Pelewan," Henry answered. "But I think that the conversation last night was too complicated for him to follow, if you're thinking that he might tell Rose was lying."

"What I mean is this," the captain said. "If Lee Boo were to come here, and I were to ask him if his father was ready for Mr. Rose to lead the men in battle, would he be able to answer in English that Aba Tuli would rather have *me* lead them?"

"Why, yes, Father. I think so," Henry answered.

"Good! If he can say that while Rose is listening, then I will have my excuse to lead the men."

"All right, sir," said Henry. "I will go to the village now and explain the mistake to Aba Tuli, and then I will bring Lee Boo back with me. I will teach him what to say on the way back."

Henry's trip to Pelew was uneventful. Aba Tuli accepted his explanation of the "mistake" the captain had made. Then Lee Boo and Henry began their trip back to camp. On the way, Henry explained to his young friend what it was the captain wanted him to say, and by the time they arrived back at the enclosure, shortly before noon, the boy understood perfectly what he was supposed to do.

During lunch, with Benger, Rose, Henry, and Lee Boo seated around him, the captain turned to Lee Boo and

142

said, "I understand that you are learning to speak English, Lee Boo."

"Yes," said Lee Boo. "I learn some."

"That's very nice." The captain was silent for a few moments as he went on eating.

As they were about to finish the meal, though, he turned again to the boy. "Is your father ready for Mr. Rose and the men to come to Pelew?" he asked.

"Yes," said Lee Boo. "But he think *you* would be better to lead the men."

The captain acted surprised, and then turned to Rose. "Well, Mr. Rose," he said. "It looks as if the king has had a change of heart, and I mustn't insult the natives by refusing to do what Aba Tuli thinks best."

Henry had been watching Rose out of the corner of his eye. He had seen the man grow pale upon hearing that Lee Boo had learned some English. When he realized that Lee Boo apparently did not understand enough of the language to be aware of his lie of the night before, his face turned an angry red at this disruption of his plans.

"No, sir," said Rose, finally. "We mustn't insult the natives."

"Very well, then, it's settled," said the captain. "Mr. Benger, you and I will lead the group. Pick about ten men to go with us. That would be two canoes full, counting paddlers, and should be plenty."

"Don't you want me to go along as interpreter?" Rose asked.

"Oh, I doubt that there will be much need for interpreting, and Lee Boo can probably handle that job all right," the captain said. "Don't you agree, Mr. Benger?"

"Aye, sir," said Benger, and he walked away to pick the men for his "army."

A short while later, the men had been chosen and issued weapons, and were ready to march to Pelew to join Aba Tuli's army. As Benger gave the order and the men marched away, the captain stopped to say goodbye to his son.

"Take care of yourself, Henry," he said. "And don't forget that tomorrow is your day to work on the canoe. Don't look for us to come back until sometime on the day after tomorrow, as we will probably spend tomorrow night on the enemy island. Now, goodbye."

"Goodbye, Father," said Henry. "Be careful, sir."

"I shall," the captain called back, waving as he walked away.

The next morning, long before dawn, some fifty of the native canoes paddled out of the harbor at Pelew. The captain and half of the Englishmen were in one large canoe, which also contained five native paddlers, and Mr. Benger and the other half of the Englishmen were in a similar canoe.

The army—or perhaps it could be better described as a navy—moved silently around the northern tip of Oroolong and then set its course due east. Just before the first light of day, half of the canoes, including the one in which Benger had his men, turned northeast away from the other half of the canoes. This unexpected splitting of forces surprised the captain.

The village which Aba Tuli intended to attack was

located on a beach which ran north and south. At the northern end of this beach, there was a point of land which stuck out about a quarter of a mile into the lagoon. The captain's group of canoes, with Aba Tuli in charge, approached the enemy village just south of this point of land. As the sun rose above the horizon, the king shouted an order, and the canoes made a wild dash for the beach.

"It's just as I thought," the captain said to his men. "We are going to charge them head-on. Be prepared to jump out and go ashore as soon as the canoe touches bottom."

Much to the captain's surprise, though, the canoes stopped about forty yards away from the beach, and the natives began hurling large stones at the houses of the village. These stones crashed through the flimsy roofs and walls of the houses, and in almost no time at all, the villagers had grabbed their weapons and were running to the beach to fight off the invaders.

Just as the enemy reached the water's edge, Aba Tuli gave a signal; his canoes turned and were paddled hastily out to sea.

"Are we just going to throw a few rocks at them and then run?" the captain exclaimed.

As he looked back toward the beach, he saw that the natives were hurriedly getting their canoes into the water. In a matter of minutes, thirty of the canoes were giving chase close on the heels of Aba Tuli's retreating forces.

As the captain's group of canoes passed the point of land, with the enemy close behind, he began to see Aba Tuli's reason for this odd battle plan. Mr. Benger's canoes, with Ara Kuka in charge, had been hidden behind that point of land, and as Aba Tuli and those who were chasing him passed beyond the point, the other group of canoes paddled in behind the enemy, cutting them off from their beach.

When Aba Tuli saw that Ara Kuka's group of canoes was in position, he ordered his canoes to turn and fight. At the same time, Benger's group engaged the enemy from the rear.

The king and Ara Kuka signaled at the same time for their English gunners to open fire. The sound of the first volley frightened the enemy so much that most of them quickly abandoned their canoes and began swimming for the point of land. The second volley sank the rest of the canoes, since Benger and the captain had ordered the muskets aimed at the boats rather than the men in them.

There was so much splashing around in the water after that that neither the captain nor the mate was able to tell whether any of the enemy had been killed or not. The natives threw their spears at the men in the water, and when all of the spears were gone, they paddled about trying to hit the swimmers with their paddles.

Finally, Aba Tuli called a halt to the fighting and had his paddlers take him into the unprotected beach. There, he jumped out of his canoe, found the enemy king's ceremonial canoe, which was kept on a scaffold near the center of the village, and set it on fire. On his way back to his own boat, he completed his revenge by setting fire to the king's house. But he did not harm any of the women or children who were running helter-skelter from one hiding place to another.

As the canoes pulled away from the beach, Aba Tuli gave the order to sail straight for the Englishmen's camp, where they arrived shortly after lunch—much to the surprise of Henry and the others who had remained behind.

"Father!" Henry shouted, as the canoes ran up onto the beach. "Was the battle called off?"

"No, my boy," laughed the captain, jumping out of his canoe. "It was simply one of the quickest battles in the history of naval warfare."

"Did you win?" Henry asked excitedly.

"Of course we won," the captain said. "Why, a master of tactics like Aba Tuli could have won easily without even having us along to help. About all we did was make a lot of noise, eh, Mr. Benger?"

"That's right, Henry," said Benger. "The king had them fooled so completely that we almost didn't get a chance to fire a shot."

The captain described the details of the battle to the rest of the men in the camp. When he had finished, they all, natives and Englishmen alike, began laughing and shouting, celebrating the victory. After a few minutes of this, though, Aba Tuli asked everyone to be quiet. Then he made a speech in which he thanked the captain and his men for helping with the battle, and he promised that he would instruct his own men to stay with the Englishmen and do whatever the captain wished, in order to help in the preparations for their departure.

The captain then complimented Aba Tuli on the way he had handled the battle, and thanked him for putting the extra men at his disposal. He told the king that if the men could gather and prepare enough food for the voyage, he thought that the Englishmen would be able to leave in five days, rather than in another week as he had planned.

Aba Tuli promised that the food would be ready and loaded aboard the finished boat by that time, and after a great deal of hand-shaking, he and Ara Kuka and a few other natives went to their canoes and rowed away, leaving the rest behind to help the Englishmen.

14

Three days later, Henry and the captain went to the village to tell Aba Tuli and Lee Boo that they would be ready to leave on the day after tomorrow.

"I have come to ask what your second request is, so that I may do whatever it is you wish before we sail," the captain said, using Henry as his interpreter.

Aba Tuli shook his head and said that he did not want to make the request until just before they were ready to depart. Then he said that he and Lee Boo would come to the encampment the next morning to see the launching of the new boat. They would spend the night in the camp, so that they would be there to say goodbye.

The captain couldn't help wondering what Aba Tuli's request might be. How could he fulfill a request if he did not know what it was until the moment before he sailed for Macao? Shaking his head, Captain Wilson said, "Well, all right. If that's the way you want it. Now come, Henry," he said. "We must return to camp, as we have a great deal to do."

"All right, Father," Henry said reluctantly, and they started back toward the camp.

"I wonder what it is that Aba Tuli wants me to do?" the captain said to Henry, as they walked through the forest.

"Perhaps he wants you to send him some tools or supplies, or even muskets like ours," Henry said.

"Possibly," said the captain. "Though I don't know why he would want to wait until the last moment to ask for such things. Of course, I couldn't predict when another ship might come this way again."

"Maybe the company will want to send a ship down here to trade for pearls," said Henry. "Then you could send some things for him."

"Yes, and he may want to give me some pearls to trade for supplies when we get back," said the captain. "Then he might want to wait until the last moment to give them to me for fear they might be stolen. Oh, well, I guess we can worry about the request *after* he makes it, can't we?" And with that, the captain lengthened his stride, and Henry almost had to run to keep up with him.

150

About the middle of the morning on the next day, Aba Tuli, Ara Kuka, Ludee, and Lee Boo arrived in camp.

It was the first time that Ludee, or any of the native women, had been to the encampment, and it was easy to see that she was very interested in all of the equipment. The cook's pots especially interested her, but unlike the native men, she went about quite silently, asking questions in a low voice and nodding pleasantly as things were explained to her. She examined the food which the natives had gathered and prepared for the Englishmen to take on their voyage and expressed her approval of the choices and methods of preparation.

The captain explained to Aba Tuli's party that the final touch, the mounting of the mast and sail, had just been completed. Everyone gathered at the prow of the great, twin-hulled boat, and the captain took a bottle of rum from his locker.

"I christen thee the *Oroolong*," the captain said, breaking the bottle on the heavy snout of one hull, and as he said these words, the men and natives put their shoulders to the prows and pushed. The *Oroolong* slid heavily through the wet sand, and then a receding wave lifted and carried her out to deeper water, where she floated evenly and steadily.

The men gave a cheer at this happy proof that their months of labor had not been in vain.

"She rides beautifully, sir," Benger said to the captain.

"Aye, that she does. She can take us all the way to Macao—even to England if she has to."

The rest of the day was spent in loading the boat with supplies that would be taken on the trip. The water kegs, the prepared food, the muskets, and the powder and ammunition, all were put into the longboat and ferried out to the *Oroolong*.

Since there was a shortage of room, though, the personal belongings of the men had to be left behind. The captain instructed his men to give their things to any of the natives who might want them. To Aba Tuli, the captain gave his clothes, and the king immediately put on one of the captain's fancy blue coats to wear in honor of the occasion.

Mr. Swift, the cook, blushed like a school girl as Ludee thanked him for the large pots which he was leaving her.

Henry gave his clothes to Lee Boo, and like Aba Tuli, he donned one of Henry's fanciest coats.

By dark, the *Oroolong* was completely loaded. Its sturdy platform, made of several crisscross layers of bamboo, was stacked high with supplies. It was then that everyone finally realized that they were actually going to leave this beautiful island the very next morning. The crew of the *Antelope* had grown to love the island, and though they were anxious to get back to their wives and sweethearts, they felt as if they were leaving friends.

"Will you come back someday, Henery?" Lee Boo asked.

"Yes," said Henry, trying to convince himself that he really might return to Oroolong one day. "I will have a ship of my own to command in a few years, and then I'll come back to see you."

"How long?" Lee Boo asked.

"Oh, ten years—or fifteen," Henry answered, realizing

that it would be an awfully long time before he could command a ship.

"You come back," Lee Boo said. "You live here. Be my brother. I give you half my islands when I am king. You be king, too."

"Yes, and then I'll have to kill a shark every year," Henry said, trying to joke.

"You strong," Lee Boo said. "You kill shark good."

"Well, we'll see," said Henry.

The next morning, just at dawn, everyone was awakened, and the final check was made to see that nothing important was being left behind. Then the men gathered at the water's edge, before climbing into the longboat which would take them to the *Oroolong*, moored some sixty or seventy yards offshore.

"Mr. Rose," the captain said. "Will you please ask Aba Tuli if he is ready to tell me what his second request is?"

Rose translated the question for Aba Tuli, and then listened patiently to the king's answer.

"My second request," said Aba Tuli, speaking in Pelewan, "is that the captain take my son, Lee Boo, to England with him, so that he may learn many new things."

Before Rose could translate the king's answer, Henry shouted excitedly, "He wants you to take Lee Boo with us!" Then he turned to Lee Boo. "Lee Boo! Lee Boo!" he shouted. "You're going with us!"

Henry stopped. He saw the grim look on the faces of the captain and the other men. Then he saw that Rose, who was standing off to one side, between the captain and himself, had a pistol in his hand.

"So young Henry understands Pelewan, does he?" Rose said. "And you knew I was lying the other night when I said that Aba Tuli wanted *me* to lead the men into battle?"

"That is correct, Mr. Rose," said the captain.

"And I suppose that my old friend Philip Benger has recognized me, too?" Rose asked.

"Yes, I remember you," said Benger, angrily. "And I've been waiting for the chance to get my hands on you."

"Well," said Rose. "You are not likely to with this gun in *my* hands. Besides, you have no argument with me. I know you think I tried to have you killed, but you are wrong. I saw you bring the bundle on deck that night, and knew what you were going to do. Since I hadn't been able to get the night watch to stay on the port side of the ship, I called his attention to the bundle you threw overboard, while you escaped. But that was long ago, and it really makes no difference now."

"May I ask what you intend to do?" interrupted the captain.

"Certainly, Captain Wilson," said Rose, with mock politeness. "I intend to take what I need of your supplies and rejoin my friends, who are holding the *Gazelle* at Yap. They would have been holding you, too, if we had not run aground."

"Then we were right," Benger said. "You were sent to lead us into a trap."

"Correct, Mr. Benger," said Rose. "Now I shall trade your supplies to the natives for passage to Yap. When I

154

get there—and by the way, Captain, even the smaller canoes such as the one the king has now will make it to Yap—when I get there, we will of course have to get rid of the *Gazelle* and her crew and sail for calmer waters.

"I am sure to get to Yap before you can hope to get to Macao—if I thought that I wouldn't, I wouldn't allow you to leave at all. So, it would be very wasteful of you to send another ship out looking for us when you get to China. We will be many miles away by the time it could reach us."

"Yes, I'm afraid you are right," the captain said.

While this conversation was going on, Henry was realizing that he was the only one in a position to keep Rose from escaping. The pirate was standing with his back partly turned toward Henry, and the boy began edging quietly around behind him, getting closer and closer as Rose talked.

At last, he was almost directly behind Rose, and only five or six paces away from him. Benger continued to ask the pirate questions to divert his attention. When Henry was three paces away from Rose, Benger stopped in the middle of a sentence and shouted, "Now, Henry!"

Henry took two great leaps toward Rose and threw his feet up into the air on a level with the pirate's shoulders, just as Rose turned to look in Henry's direction. Henry kicked both feet with all his might, knocking Rose sprawling in the sand.

Benger grabbed the pistol. The pirate got slowly to his hands and knees, shaking his head. He looked up into the muzzle of his own pistol.

155

"Captain," said Benger. "I suggestion that we tie Mr. Rose up so that he will cause no more trouble."

Then he turned to Henry who was picking himself up off of the ground. "Well done, Henry," he said. "I knew you could do it."

Rose was tied up and placed in the longboat. The captain turned back to Aba Tuli, who was completely bewildered by what had taken place. He explained briefly what had caused the trouble, and then returned to the topic of the king's second request.

"We shall be very happy to take Lee Boo with us, Aba Tuli," the captain said, using Henry as his interpreter. "He will learn many things in England that will be of great use to him when he becomes king of these islands."

Aba Tuli dug into a large woven pouch which he had brought with him and pulled out another bag about the size of the crown of a man's hat. He opened this bag and showed the captain that it was full of pearls.

"You say that these are very valuable in your country," he said. "Will this many of them be enough for Lee Boo to trade for what he will need in England?"

"Why, yes," said the captain, a little awed by the sight of so many pearls. "He will be one of the wealthiest boys in all England."

"Then you keep them for him," said Aba Tuli, handing the bag to Captain Wilson. "But give some to your men and to Henry. Now go before the tide runs out."

The surprised Lee Boo took the large pouch which Ludee had secretly packed for him, and which contained all the things she thought he might need. Then he said to

156

his mother and father, "Henry is my brother, now, and we will both return to Oroolong when I have learned enough."

"Yes," said Aba Tuli. "You will both be great kings when you return."

And Ludee, just as any English mother would have done, shook her finger at her son, as tears streamed down her cheeks. "You be good," she said.

Everyone clambered aboard the longboat as it was shoved into the water. After a few swift paddle strokes by the natives to whom the boat was being left, they climbed from it onto the *Oroolong*. Then, as the natives rowed the long boat back to the beach, the sail was raised on the *Oroolong*, the anchor was lifted, and the large boat began to drift away swiftly on the outgoing tide.

"Set your course for the opening in the reef, Mr. Benger," said the captain. "And then set your course for Macao."

"Aye, aye, sir," the mate answered. He and the captain smiled at each other, both of them glad to feel a deck under their feet again.

15

The *Oroolong* sailed from the island for which it was named on Wednesday, November 12, 1783. Henry found the double-hulled boat very exciting for the first few days. It did not roll or pitch nearly so much as the *Antelope* had, and he enjoyed sitting in one hull and watching the other hull knife through the water.

Also, during these days, he and Lee Boo resumed their studies of each other's language. Between lessons, they lay on the platform of the boat and dangled Lee Boo's bone fishhooks in the water. But though they caught an occasional fish, both boys were beginning to get somewhat bored with the voyage as the first week drew to a close.

Each day at noon, Mr. Benger would stand on the platform and take a reading of their position. One week from the day that they left Oroolong, he called the captain to him.

"Sir," he said, "I suspected this on our fourth day out, but I wanted to verify my readings thoroughly before I mentioned it to you. Now I think that there is no doubt about it."

"What is it, Mr. Benger?" the captain asked, a worried look coming to his face.

"If my readings are correct, Captain," said Benger, "we are sailing at about twice the rate of speed that we had expected to."

"Impossible!" exclaimed the captain. "This boat can't travel more than twice as fast as the *Antelope*."

"Mr. Benger is right, Captain," said Rose, who had been untied two or three days after they had sailed. "These twin-hulled boats are the fastest vessels I have ever seen anywhere, and they will sail rings around any European ship that was ever built."

"And where do your readings say we are now, Mr. Benger?" the captain asked.

"Just about here," Benger answered, pointing to a spot on the captain's chart. "Off the east coast of the Philippines."

The captain did some rapid calculations in his head, and then stared at Benger. "At that rate, we will make

160

the passage from Oroolong to Macao in only eighteen days!"

"That's right, sir," Benger said. "In eleven days from now we should be there, if our wind keeps up."

"We are far enough north now that we might see another ship, too," said the captain, "so we had better start posting a watch to keep a lookout. Though this is a good boat, I would still feel much safer aboard a more familiar type of vessel."

"Aye, aye, sir," said Benger, and he began letting the men know when each one would stand his watch.

"Mr. Rose, now that there is a possibility that we will meet another ship and be taken aboard her, there is something I want to talk to you about," the captain said.

"All right, Captain," said Rose.

"When we get to Macao," said the captain, "it will probably be possible for the East India Company to send a man-of-war to Yap to try to capture your friends."

"Yes, that's true," Rose agreed.

"But if a man-of-war is sent to do the job," continued the captain, "the pirates would recognize it as a warship and have plenty of time to kill the people who were on the *Gazelle*, or at least they could hold them as hostages and still make their escape."

"That's true, too," said Rose.

"If a merchant ship were sent to Yap, though, and if you were to go ashore and tell your friends that you had captured that ship with the help of a mutinous crew," said the captain, "then that ship could sail right into the harbor and capture the pirates while their guard was down, couldn't it?"

161

"Yes, I suppose it could," Rose said.

"Mind you I can make no promises," said the captain, "but if you were to agree to assume that pose and help the Company to capture the pirates and recover the *Gazelle*, I am sure the officials of the Company could arrange for you to be given a full pardon for your past activities. You seem to be a very intelligent man, and I shouldn't be surprised if the Company might even find a good position for you. Now, what do you say to that?"

"Well, Captain," said Rose. "It seems like a very good arrangement to me."

"Very well, then," said the captain. "All that I can promise you is that I will do everything I can."

"Thank you, Captain," Rose said. "I understand your position, and I am willing to take my chances that the officials will agree to such a bargain."

"Good! Then it's settled," the captain said.

On their twelfth day at sea, the lookout on the *Oroolong* sighted a sail far to the north of them.

"What course is she taking and what is her nationality, Mr. Benger?" the captain asked.

"Her course seems to be northwest, sir," Benger said, focusing his glass on the ship. "And I believe she is English."

"Can we catch her?" the captain asked.

"I doubt that we can before dark, sir," Benger said. "But perhaps we can get close enough so that they will hear a musket if we fire one. They might stay in the area until morning to investigate."

"It's our only chance, I suppose. Let's get as close to her as we possibly can," the captain said.

For the rest of the afternoon, the *Oroolong* sailed rapidly in the direction of the ship. When darkness was beginning to fall, the captain ordered a musket fired once every minute during the few minutes of light which were left.

"We must stay in this area now until dawn, Mr. Benger," the captain said when night had fallen. "We don't want to sail off and leave them in the dark."

"Aye, aye, sir," said Benger. "It's a shame we were not able to have at least a lantern of some sort aboard."

"Yes, it is too bad," agreed the captain. "But any fire would have been extremely dangerous to have around this bamboo."

All hands were awake and on the lookout for the ship when dawn broke the next morning, but though they strained their eyes until long after full daylight had come, there was no sign of her.

"Well, we have lost enough time," the captain said. "If we had continued on course, we would have beaten them to Macao, if that is where they are going."

"Aye, aye, sir," said Benger, and he again set the course for Macao.

Late the next morning, Mr. Benger stepped up to the platform to take his daily reading of their position. He called the figures off to the captain, who jotted them down on the chart. The captain asked him to take a second reading to be sure that the first one was correct.

Benger again began sighting the sun, but a sudden gust of wind brought the sail around to block his way.

He took a few steps back to get the sun in his sights again.

"Look out!" shouted Henry, who had been watching, but his warning came too late. Benger had fallen off the platform.

Rose, who was in the stern of one of the canoes, threw a rope which just barely reached the mate. Benger grabbed it and was quickly pulled into the boat.

"My instruments!" he shouted. "I had the sextant and compass in my hands when I fell overboard!"

"We could have done without the sextant, since we know our present position, but with no compass there is no telling where we might go!" the captain exclaimed.

"Well," said Benger, beginning to calm down, "they are both gone, so we will just have to do our best without them."

"Do you think you can get us to Macao by using the sun and the North Star?" the captain asked.

"I can get us to the coast of China," said Benger, "but I can't guarantee what part of the coast."

"That won't be much help," the captain said. "While we're wandering around looking for a friendly port, we could be robbed and killed by bandits."

"Wait a moment," Benger said suddenly. "Do you suppose Lee Boo knows enough about navigating by the stars to take us to a place he has never been to before?"

"I doubt it," the captain said, "but there would be no harm in asking him." He turned and called to Lee Boo, who was in the other hull.

"Lee Boo, can you take us by the stars to this place?" He pointed to the map.

164

Lee Boo looked at the map for a few moments, and then pointed his finger at the mark which the captain had made from the reading Benger had given him just before falling overboard. "We here?" he asked.

"Yes," said the captain.

Lee Boo pointed at the spot indicated by the captain as Macao. "We go there?" he asked.

"Yes," said the captain.

"All right," said Lee Boo, and he climbed back to the platform. For some moments, the boy stood there looking around at the sky. Then he walked to the tiller and told the helmsman, "You go. I do this."

The sailor, not knowing what to do, looked over at the captain, who called to him, "Let him take the tiller."

Lee Boo sat down with the tiller under his arm and calmly took charge of the boat.

"Does he intend to sit there until we get to Macao?" Benger asked.

"I don't know, but perhaps I had better tell him that we are four days away from there, and that he will have to let some of the others handle the boat part of the time," the captain answered. He walked back to Lee Boo, and with Henry's help, explained.

But Lee Boo had agreed to take the boat to Macao, and he intended to do just that, so he simply stared past them at the horizon and kept repeating, "I do this."

All day every day, and all night every night, Lee Boo sat at the tiller, getting up only a few times at night to walk to the platform, where he could get a better view of the stars. He would stand for a while looking into the heavens, and then he would go back to the tiller, change

165

their course ever so slightly, and sit staring straight ahead, as though he were in a trance.

As darkness fell on the fourth night, the captain spoke to Mr. Benger. "I don't see how that boy has kept himself awake for four days and four nights," he said.

"Well, sir, I only hope that he *hasn't* gone to sleep since he's been at that tiller," Benger said.

"What do you mean?" the captain asked.

"Well, sir," said Benger, "I was almost sure that we were going to sight land today, and none has come into view."

"Any number of things could have kept us from making it, Mr. Benger. Our speed might have fallen off, or we might have entered a current. I can't believe Lee Boo wouldn't tell us if he did not know where we are."

"I hope you're right, sir," said Benger. "Since the boy has never seen a city, though, I suggest that all hands stay awake tonight, just to be certain that we don't pass right by Macao."

"That's a good idea, Mr. Benger," said the captain. "You may give orders to that effect."

But the voyage had been a long and tiresome one, and by four o'clock the next morning, everyone on the *Oroolong* had dropped off to sleep except Lee Boo; he had fought off sleep for more than a hundred hours. So on into the night, the boat sailed, with Lee Boo's eyes alone peering into the darkness.

It was after daylight the next morning when the captain and Mr. Benger were awakened by Lee Boo's voice calling to them, "We go here? We go here?"

Benger raised up and looked over the edge of the

166

canoe. Then he sat bolt upright and looked all around him. "Blast me, Captain!" he cried. "The little blighter has sailed us straight into the harbor!"

The captain turned toward the tiller. "Lee Boo . . ." He stopped, for Lee Boo, his job done, was fast asleep.

16

As soon as the awakened crew had worked the *Oroolong* into a dock, a runner was sent to the East India Company with word that the men of the *Antelope* had returned. Then the men climbed out of their boat and began to exercise. They had been cooped up in the narrow hulls for a long time.

"Men," said the captain, gathering his crew around him, "I think that we could all use a long walk. I suggest that we start in that direction and meet the Company officials halfway."

"Captain, have you forgotten that this is Sunday?" asked Benger. "No one will be at the office."

"I had forgotten," said the captain. "But, yes, someone will be there. Someone is always on duty."

The men began walking up the street, passing the growing crowd which had gathered to see this strange group of men and their odd-looking boat. They had gone only a few blocks when they met Mr. Bruce, one of the two men who had seen them off the day the *Antelope* sailed from Macao. He was breathless, having run all the way from the office. "What is the trouble? What are you doing back here? Did you find the *Gazelle*?"

"No, we didn't find the *Gazelle*," said the captain. "But we know where she is, and we have a man who will help get her back."

"Get her back?" said Mr. Bruce. "What do you mean?"

"She has been captured by pirates," the captain explained, "but she's safe and so is her crew."

"But what are you doing in this condition?" Bruce asked, indicating the unkempt appearance of the men.

"We have been marooned on an island for four months," said the captain.

"Where is the *Antelope*?" Mr. Bruce asked before the captain could say anything else.

"The *Antelope* is at the bottom of the Pacific Ocean," the captain said. "And if you don't stop asking questions and show us where we can rest, I will very likely send you down to find her."

"Oh," said Bruce, finally realizing that the men must have gone through a great deal. "Come with me, all of you. Mr. Lane lives only a short distance from here, and you can rest there."

When the men arrived at Lane's house, he, too, began

asking questions. Bruce stopped him, though, and together with the servants, they fixed a place for every man
to rest while a hot meal was being prepared for them.
After almost three weeks of raw fruit and vegetables and
salted fish, the hot food tasted so good the men almost
gorged themselves on it.

For the rest of the day, they were allowed to eat and
sleep as much as they wished, and by the time night
came, they were feeling quite well again. After supper,
the captain told Bruce and Lane that he was ready to
relate all that had happened. Benger, Henry, and Lee
Boo were shown into the study, along with the captain.

The captain introduced Lee Boo and then sent the boy
off to bed, since he was almost asleep on his feet. Then,
for the next three hours, he told them of the shipwreck,
their encounter with the natives, and how they became
friends. He ended his story by explaining who Rose
was, and the bargain he had promised the pirate he
would try to get the Company to make.

"There is a man-of-war in the harbor at present," said
Bruce. "But you don't think we should send it to rescue
the crew of the *Gazelle*?"

"Not if you value the lives of those men," the captain
said. "The only way to get them back safely is by trick-
ing the pirates."

"Well, then," said Lane. "I should say that settles it.
If Rose helps us to get the crew back safely, we will see
to it that he gets a full pardon, and we will give him a
job, too. We can certainly use a good linguist."

"Excellent!" said the captain. "And now I think that

171

we had better get more sleep. We have a great deal of catching up to do."

The next few days were ones of endless excitement for Lee Boo. Everything was new to him. He had never seen tables, chairs, windows, horses, dogs, cats, carriages—in fact, there was hardly anything present that he *had* seen before. So he was quite unhappy when Henry told him one afternoon that they were to leave Macao the next morning aboard the man-of-war.

But when Henry explained to him that they would be sailing in a warship, and that there were even more exciting things to see in England, he became completely happy.

The next day, December 7, 1783, eight months from the time they had sailed from England, and about the date on which the captain had originally hoped to arrive back in England, they set sail a second time from Macao. Lee Boo, the officers, and the midshipmen of the *Antelope* were passengers this time. The ordinary seamen had been left behind to work their way home on other merchant ships of the Company. This pleased them all, as it meant a vacation with pay before they had to work again.

Lee Boo and Henry were standing at the stern of the man-of-war that morning as it glided gently out of the harbor, its huge sails billowing in the breeze. They were watching the buildings grow smaller as the ship moved away from the land, and didn't hear Captain Wilson walk up behind them.

"Well, lad," the captain said, as he put his arm around Henry's shoulders, "we're off for home again. Was this voyage adventurous enough for you?"

172

"Oh, I suppose so," said Henry. Then he looked at his father and grinned broadly.

The captain smiled back at him and laughed, and both of them turned to gaze at Lee Boo. He was standing with his feet firmly planted on the deck and his hands clasped behind his back, looking over the man-of-war with an appraising eye. *"Weel! Weel a trecoy!"* he said.

"Thank goodness he approves of the British Navy," said Henry.